Tanith Lee

BLACK UNICORN

TANITH LEE is one of the leading writers of her generation. Born and raised in England, her elegant science fiction, fantasy, horror, mainstream and juvenile novels and short stories have earned her a huge following. Despite her many excellent forays into other fields, though, it is her fantasy novels which remain best known—titles such as *Vazkor, Son of Vazkor*; *Lycanthia*; and *Anackire*. She is a winner of the British Fantasy Award, the SF Chronicle Award, and a two-time winner of the World Fantasy Award, and was dubbed "Princess Royal of Fantasy" by Dutch publisher Meulenhoff.

HEATHER COOPER is a Canadian artist, best known for her finely detailed paintings in mythical romantic themes. In 1987 she published *Carneval Perpetual*, a retrospective book of her paintings, illustrations, and design. She resides in Toronto, Canada, and is the principal of Heather Cooper Communication by Design, Ltd., specializing in graphic design and illustration.

ALSO AVAILABLE
Fantasies published by ibooks, inc.:

Nightwings
by Robert Silverberg

Roger Zelazny's The Dawn of Amber
by John Gregory Betancourt

The Roadkill of Middle Earth
by John Carnell
Illustrated by Tom Sutton

ROGER ZELAZNY COLLECTIONS
The Doors of His Face, The Lamps of His Mouth
The Last Defender of Camelot

BLACK UNICORN

Tanith Lee

Illustrated by
Heather Cooper

ibooks

DISTRIBUTED BY PUBLISHERS GROUP WEST

A Publication of ibooks, inc.

An ibooks, inc. Book
Published through arrangement with
Byron Preiss Visual Publications, Inc.

Distributed by Publishers Group West
1700 Fourth Street, Berkeley, CA 94710

ibooks, inc.
24 West 25th Street
New York, NY 10010

ISBN 1-59687-162-8
First ibooks, inc. printing December 2002
Second ibooks, inc. printing December 2005
10 9 8 7 6 5 4 3 2

Edited by David M. Harris

Special thanks to Jonathan Lanman,
David Keller, and John Betancourt

Cover painting by Heather Cooper
Cover design by Mike Rivilis
Interior design by Paula Keller and Linda Roppolo

Printed in the U.S.A.

To
Louise Cooper,
Maker of stories, singer of unicorns

PART

One

1

The first thing Tanaquil saw almost every morning on waking was her mother's face. But that was because a painting of Tanaquil's mother, the sorceress Jaive, hung opposite the bed. The painting of Jaive had a great bush of scarlet hair in which various jewels, plants, implements, and mice and other small animals she used in her researches were caught. "Good morning, Mother," said Tanaquil to the picture, and the picture vigorously answered: "Rise with the sun, salute the day!" As it always did. Since it was anyway usually midmorning when Tanaquil woke up, the greeting was completely unsuitable.

Once the business with the picture was over, Tanaquil got out of bed and went to see what had been left for her breakfast. Sometimes nothing had. Today there were some pieces of cold toasted bread without any butter, an orange, and green herbal tea in a glass. Tanaquil tried the tea, then peeled the orange cautiously. As she split the segments a bird flew out.

"This way, this way," said Tanaquil impatiently to the bird as it dashed round the room, sticking its beak into the bed curtains. The bird hurtled to the window and flew into the hard red sunshine. Tanaquil stood at the window, looking away across the roofs and battlements of her mother's fortress, at the desert. It was the same view she had seen since she could remember. For nearly sixteen years this had been her bedroom and that had been the view. The long tawny sands, with their glints of minerals, which changed shape after the wind blew, the march of rock hills half a mile off, some pointed like cones, some with great natural archways that ran through them, showing the endlessness of the desert beyond. From any part of Jaive's fortress, if you looked out, this was the kind of thing you saw, dunes and rocks, and the hot sky. By day the fortress and the desert baked. At night it grew cold and a thin snow fell, the sand turned to silver and the stars burned white.

"Hey," said a high-pitched voice outside, "hey."

Tanaquil glanced and saw one of the peeves was sitting on the roof below her window. It was about the size of a large cat, with thick brown fur over a barrel-shaped body and short muscular legs. It gripped with three paws and with the fourth scratched itself busily. It had a long dainty muzzle, a bushy tail, and ears that would go up in points, although just now they flopped down. In its big yellow eyes was an urgent look.

"Want a bone," said the peeve.

"I'm sorry I haven't got one," said Tanaquil.

"No, no, want a *bone*," insisted the peeve. It hopped up the roof and jumped into the embrasure of the window like a fat fur pig. Tanaquil put out her hand to stroke the peeve, but it evaded her and plopped down into the room. It began to hurry about scratching at things and poking its long nose under the rug, upsetting the stool. It pattered across Tanaquil's work table, through her collection of easily damaged fossils, and over a small clock lying on its back. The peeve scattered cogs and wheels. It sprang. Now it was in the fireplace.

"There are no bones *here*," said Tanaquil firmly.

The peeve took no notice. "Want a bone," it explained, and knocked over her breakfast. The herbal tea spread across the floor, and the peeve drank it, sneezing and snuffling. A piece of toast had fallen on its head, and it threw it off with an irritated *"Bone, bone."*

Tanaquil sighed. She went into the marble bath alcove and pressed the head of the lion for a fountain of cool water to wash in. The water did not come. Instead a stream of sticky berry wine poured out.

"Oh, *Mother!*" shouted Tanaquil, furiously. She ran out, kicked the stool across the room, and then the pieces of bread. The orange had turned into a sort of flower that was growing up the left-hand pillar of the fireplace. The peeve was nibbling this. It turned and watched as Tanaquil dressed herself in yesterday's crumpled dress and ran a comb through her hair, which was a lighter red than Jaive's.

"Got a bone?"

"I haven't got a bone for heaven's sake! Be quiet."

The peeve sat down and washed its stomach, now muttering anxiously, "Flea, flea." Then abruptly it threw itself up the chimney and was gone, although a shower of soot fell down into the hearth.

Tanaquil left the room a moment after, slamming the door.

Four flights of wide stone stairs, with wooden bannisters carved with beasts, fruits, demons and so on, went up from Tanaquil's level to the haunt of her mother. On each landing there was an opening to the roof walks and battlements, and in one place Tanaquil saw three of the soldiers sitting on the wall playing a game of Scorpions and Ladders. They were all drunk, as usual, but, noting Tanaquil passing, one called out: "Don't go up, Lady. The sorceress is busy."

"Unfortunate," said Tanaquil. And she climbed the last flight, out of breath, and reached the big black door that shut off her mother's Sorcerium.

In the center of the door was a head of green jade, which addressed Tanaquil. "Do you seek Jaive?"

"Obviously."

"What is your name, and rank?"

"Tanaquil, her daughter."

The head seemed to purse its lips, but then the door gave a creak and swung massively open.

The chamber beyond was full of oily smoke and pale lightning flashes. Tanaquil was used to this. She walked in and found her way among looming chests and stands cluttered with objects, some of which cheeped and chittered. Suddenly there was a great mirror, and in it Tanaquil caught a glimpse of a burning city, towers and sparks and creatures flying through the air. Then the vision vanished, and the smoke sank. Jaive appeared out of the sinking smoke. She stood behind a table covered with books, globes of glass, instruments, wands, and colored substances that bubbled. In a large cage sat two white mice with rabbit ears and the tails of serpents, eating a sausage. Jaive wore a floor-length gown of black-green silk sewn with golden embroidery. Her flaming hair surrounded her face like the burning city in the mirror. She frowned.

"What do you want?" asked Tanaquil's mother.

"Would you like a list?" said Tanaquil.

"I am engaged—" said Jaive.

"You always are. Did you enjoy your breakfast, mother? Mine had a bird in it and then turned into a flower. One of the peeves spilled the rest. My fountain water was berry wine. Most of my clothes have disappeared. *I'm sick of it!*"

"What is this nonsense?" said Jaive.

"Mother, you know that everything is in an eternal mess here because of your magic, because of leaks of power and side effects of incantations. It's awful."

"I search for knowledge," said Jaive. She added vaguely, "How dare you speak to your mother like this?"

Tanaquil sat down on a large dog of some kind that had temporarily turned into a stool.

"When I was little," said Tanaquil, "I thought it was wonderful. When you made the butterflies come out of the fire, and when you made the garden grow in the desert. But the butterflies went pop and the garden dissolved."

"These childish memories," said Jaive. "I've tried to educate you in the art of sorcery."

"And I wasn't any good at it," said Tanaquil.

"Dreadful," agreed her mother. "You're a mere mechanical, I'm afraid." She made a pass over a beaker and a tiny storm rose into the air. Jaive laughed in pleasure. Tanaquil's stomach rumbled.

"Mother," said Tanaquil, "perhaps I should leave."

"Yes, do, Tanaquil. Let me get on."

"I mean leave the fortress."

"Tiresome girl, where could you go?"

Tanaquil said, warily, "If my father—"

Jaive swelled; her robe billowed and her eyes flashed; small faces, imps perhaps, or only tangles, looked out of her hair.

"I have never told you who your father was. I renounced him. I know nothing of him now. Perhaps he no longer lives."

"After all," said Tanaquil, "I hardly ever see you, you wouldn't miss me. And he—"

"I won't discuss it. I've told you before, your father is nothing to me. You must put him out of your mind."

Tanaquil lost her temper again. She stood up and glared at the mice's sausage.

"Perhaps I'll just go anyway. Anywhere must be better!"

"It would take days to cross the desert, stupid child. Only a sorceress could manage it."

"Then help me."

"I wish you to remain here. You're my daughter."

There was a rattling noise in the wall, and a faint soprano voice came down to them from near the ceiling. ". . . *Bone* . . ." The peeve was passing on its quest through the chimneys.

Jaive took little notice. The peeves, desert animals that had made burrows about her fort, thinking it another rock, had years before been infected by her magic and so begun to speak. To Tanaquil the peeve symbolized everything that was wrong. She said tensely, "Mother, you must let me go."

"No," said Jaive. And with tiger's eyes she smiled on her daughter.

Tanaquil got up from the dog and went back across the room and out of the door. On the green jade head, at the age of twelve, she had once painted a moustache, and the head had blinked a ray at her that threw her down the stairs. Tanaquil closed the black door restrainedly and wondered where to vent her anger and frustration.

Jaive's fortress had been built in the time of her grandmother, also a sorceress and recluse. It was a strange building of rather muddled design, and from a distance on the desert it was not only peeves who thought it only a peculiar formation of rock. To reach the kitchen of the fort, it was necessary to roam through several long and winding corridors and then down a gloomy cavernous stair into the basement. This Tanaquil did.

In the third corridor, a carved gargoyle on a beam, touched by another random breath of Jaive's magic, abruptly flared its wings and crowed, but Tanaquil ignored it. She carried the small clock she had been repairing for the cook. This was something Tanaquil was good at. Since the age of ten, she had found herself able to mend things. And so, while her mother extravagantly summoned and questioned demons in her Sorcerium, Tanaquil worked carefully on broken dolls and clocks, music boxes, and even sometimes some of the soldiers' crossbows, or bits of the cannon, which were never used except by accident and often went wrong.

The kitchen lay six feet below ground, with high windows near the ceiling that let in the light and the sand. Boys were supposed to be constantly at work, sweeping the floors or brushing off the surfaces. On approaching the kitchen, though, it was usually remarkable only for its stillness and the lazy buzz of talk.

Tanaquil opened the door.

The cook sat on her chair with her feet on the row of ovens, most of which were cold. Two scullery maids were playing Scorpions and Ladders, and the third was embroidering. None of the sweeper boys was present. A large pot of yellow tea was on the table, and a plate of pancakes.

"Here's your clock," said Tanaquil, delivering it. She took a pancake and poured herself some tea.

"There now. It goes. Just look. What a clever lady."

"Is there anything else that wants mending?" asked Tanaquil. For five years, this was all that had stopped her from going mad, she thought. And there always was something. But as if out of spite the cook shook her shaggy head. "Not a thing. And that doll you saw to for Pillow's child is still lovely, moving its arms and going *Mamaa!*"

"And she's tried ever so hard to break it again," said Pillow, the embroiderer.

"Well, if there's nothing," said Tanaquil, trying to sound businesslike. She felt dejected.

"Let's see," said the cook, "would the lady like to make a cake?"

Tanaquil fought with a blush. "No, thank you." The cook had comforted Tanaquil when she was little, letting her make iced biscuits and gingerbread camels in the ovens, to keep her from being bored and lonely. But this was not the answer now. Even mending something was not, although it would have helped. "I'll be on my way," said Tanaquil airily.

As she closed the kitchen door, she heard the cook say to Pillow, "Madam really ought to have done something with that girl, it's a waste."

A waste, thought Tanaquil as she went back up the stairs from the kitchen. *I've been wasted.* And she shouted at a large rat that was quietly coming down. The rats had never been infected with magical speech, or never bothered to use it if they had. Nevertheless it looked offended.

Tanaquil climbed again up the fortress. She now seemed to herself to have spent most of her days going up and down and around it. She came out on one of the lower battlements, where the captain of the soldiers had his apartment in a turret. In fact he was out on the wall walk with four of his men, rolling wooden balls at a mark.

"It's the young lady," said one of the soldiers.

They all straightened up and saluted her.

The captain offered her his beer flagon, but she refused.

"Nothing to repair," said the captain. "You may have heard the cannon go off last week—Borrik thought he saw an army coming, but it was that dust storm, of course. Even so, the machine worked a treat, thanks to that hinge you saw to."

"Oh," said Tanaquil. "And the bows?"

"First class. Even Iggel's throw-knife works, after you fixed the balance. I expect something or other will go wrong in a day or so," he added encouragingly.

Tanaquil had a sudden humiliating idea that some of the kinder soldiers might muck up their equipment simply in order to give her something to do.

"What a relief," said Tanaquil. "A free afternoon at last!" And she sauntered off.

The other occasional thing Tanaquil had been doing over the weeks, months, years of her life in Jaive's fortress, had been to go for a Walk. Her first memories of Walks were that her nurse—naturally, Jaive had had little time to spare—took Tanaquil up and down all the corridors, and sometimes out into the inner courtyard, which was quite large, and planted with orange trees, grapevines, laurel hedges, and one dusty dilapidated palm only thirteen feet high. At one end of the yard was a kitchen garden, rather overgrown, some grass where goats were penned, and an ornate stone well on which was a stone eagle. Now and then the eagle changed shape, and it was always the first thing the little Tanaquil ran to see: Once it had looked like an ostrich. Then Tanaquil would play in the courtyard, alone but for the nurse, for there had been no children anywhere near her own age. As Tanaquil grew older, and the nurse more elderly, the Walks wended outside the fortress. In the beginning Tanaquil had been very interested in the desert. She had made sand castles of neater appearance than the fortress. But beyond the shadow of the fortress's walls, the dunes blistered. There was no oasis for miles, no village. The fort contained the only water. When she was older still, Tanaquil used to set out for the rock hills. The nurse never made it so far, and used to stand feebly calling on the sand, under her parasol. Tanaquil was twelve before she managed to get to the rocks. Her triumph was marred because there was absolutely nothing on the other side but more sand exactly the same as the rest, stretching away and away to the lavender horizon.

Now Tanaquil went for a Walk every other day, solely to ease her restlessness with exercise. The Walk was completely boring and purposeless. But to do it she must put on boots against the burning sand and cover her red head with a silk scarf tied with a band of ribbon. She would walk as far as the rock hills, sit in their shade, and drink some water she had brought with her. Sometimes she climbed their sides, and dug out small, frail fossils with her knife. Then perhaps she would walk a mile or so further off, west, across the sands. When she did this she fantasized to herself that she was leaving home. That just out of sight was a mighty city of tiled walls, domes and gardens, fountains, markets and noisy crowds. But she knew from the lessons her mother had given her for an hour every day until she was fourteen, that although there was a city, it was a hundred miles off. Nor in all her life had Tanaquil ever seen a caravan cross the desert near Jaive's fortress. They did not come this way. Strangers were limited to desert traders, herders, and wild dogs and jackals. Near sunset, Tanaquil would face up to facts, turn round, and come back from the desert.

Today Tanaquil went for a Walk.

As she plodded across the sand, skidded down dunes, she was entirely occupied with questions. Had yesterday been so different from all the other days? Had she felt, yesterday, this terrific urge, much more than fantasy, to escape? It was as if, like the eagle, she had changed shape overnight. Now she was someone else, another, desperate Tanaquil.

But it was impossible. She must get away—and she could not.

Some peeves were romping near the base of the rock hills. They gave off loud raucous squeaks, and Tanaquil realized they had not caught the magic speech.

She drank the water from her bottle, then got up the hill formed like a bridge, nearly flat at the top, and with the great hollow arch beneath. She sat on the bridge-hill and looked at all the old scrapings her own knife had made. There was one small fossil left, a pale shell, but so delicate it would crack if she cut down for it.

Tanaquil stared out instead over the sand. Gradually a mirage came to be, of a river with trees on its banks.

Once the whole desert had been covered by the sea, which had left behind the shells and skeletons of weird creatures now extinct. One night, Jaive had shown Tanaquil an illusion of the sea on the desert. The waves had swirled about the fortress, frosted at the top with foam, and the moon shone redder than the sun.

"You must remember," said Jaive to the nine-year-old

Tanaquil, "that this world is badly made. But we sorcerers believe there are other worlds, some worse, and one the improved
model of this. Of this perfect world we may catch glimpses."
And she had tried to teach Tanaquil use of the magic mirror, but
Tanaquil had made a mistake and the mirror cracked and Jaive
had been furious.

"Oh, Mother," said Tanaquil.

She sat on the bridge-rock until the sun began to wester over
the sloping dunes. Then she got up and faced back toward the
fortress of the sorceress.

Probably she could find some cold snacks in the kitchen.
There was seldom dinner in her mother's hall. Then she must
search the library for a readable book—though bursting with
volumes, the library had few of these. And then. What was there
but to go to bed and sleep as long as she could?

Tanaquil went up to her room from the library, where she
had read part of a book on ancient witchcraft and part of a
parchment on sorcerer-princes, having located nothing else. She
had decided to try to find some of her missing clothes, which
usually moved themselves into absurd places, such as up the
chimney, or mixed themselves with the furnishings and changed
color, so that they blended.

As she was investigating the chimney, Tanaquil recalled the
peeve that had rushed up there after a bone. She hoped it had
found a way out. Although the nights were icy cold, fires were
not often lit. Tanaquil, in passing, pressed the lion's mouth for
hot water, but a fountain of paper flowers fell out.

Beyond the window, light snow drifted to the desert. The
moon had risen, and the dunes were iced biscuits.

Tanaquil looked at her bed.

On the pillows lay something round and black. Tanaquil
approached with caution. "*Oh*, no!" shouted Tanaquil. "You
wretched thing!"

The peeve of the morning—covered thick with the black soot
it had also sprinkled generously all over the bed and the pillows,
which it had also decorated with black paw marks—raised its
head.

"What?" asked the peeve.

"Just look what you've done, you pest."

"Done nothing," said the peeve. "What done?" It looked
about, surprised.

"All this ghastly mess—"

"Soots," said the peeve. "Wash, wash," and it rolled about, licking itself halfheartedly, spreading the soot further.

Tanaquil grabbed the peeve and bore it to the window. She plumped it in the embrasure and gave its flank a sharp tap. "Get out. Go away."

"Moon," said the peeve, staring rapturously skyward.

"Go *away.*"

Tanaquil slammed the shutters on it.

She dreamed she was running over the dunes, in the snow. Her feet were bare, she went like the wind. There were no rocks, no sign of the fortress, she did not know where she was and did not care.

She woke up because of a loud rasping and scratching on the shutters.

"Come in," stated a voice, "come in now."

"Go away," repeated Tanaquil to the peeve.

But the peeve went on scratching and demanding to enter.

"If I come to the window, I'll push you off onto the roof below," threatened Tanaquil.

"Come in," said the peeve. "Now."

Tanaquil got up scowling. She flung the shutters wide. There, in a glistening oval of moonshine, crouched the peeve. "Bone," said the peeve to her intently, *"found* a bone."

And it nosed something on the stone at its paw.

Tanaquil gazed. What she had taken for a bar of moonlight was not. It was a bone. Long and slender, unhuman, not at once identifiable, the material from which it was made glowed like polished milk-crystal. And in the crystal were tiny blazing specks and glints, like diamond—no, like the stars out of the sky.

"A *bone?*" whispered Tanaquil. "Where did you find it?"

"*Found* it," said the peeve.

"But *where?*"

"Sandy," said the peeve, "hot." It blinked and took the bone lightly up again into its mouth.

Tanaquil reached out to touch. The peeve growled around the bone and lashed its tail, making a thumping noise on the shutters. "*Mine.*"

"Yes, I know it's yours. But you brought it to show me. Let me—"

"Rrr," said the peeve.

It backed away, the incredible tube of starlight gleaming between its teeth.

"You mustn't—don't *crunch* it—" cried Tanaquil.

The peeve wrinkled its face and abruptly threw itself around, in a kind of horizontal somersault. It fled, fur rippling, tail flapping, scuttling and rolling along the roof below, and vanished over an ornamental weathervane into the confused stages of darkness beneath.

2

Morning was still dim in the kitchen. The oil lamps burned and the cook was taking her hair out of its pins, while Pillow bathed her child in the sink.

Tanaquil advanced and, bravely opening the pail for the rubbish heap, began to rummage.

"Why, whatever are you after, Lady?"

"I'm looking for a nice juicy meat bone."

Pillow gave a faint shriek.

The cook said winningly, "Now, Lady. Just you wait, and I'll do you some fried bread—"

"No, it's a bone I want, with some good bits of meat still on it—roasted or raw, I don't mind."

"Poor girl," said Pillow.

"There's been nothing like that for a month," said the cook, "not since the last dinner in hall. Is it the marrow you're after, for soup?"

"It isn't for me," said Tanaquil, irritated. The pail contained peelings and eggshells, moldy crusts and other unpleasant debris. No bones and no remnants of meat. She knew quite well the kitchen usually made itself a huge roast joint once a week, but perhaps they had been too lazy recently. "What have you got? Meat fat? Put that on some toast, thickly, for me—and a bowl of that green tea."

"Green?" The cook shook her hair-knots. "There's no green tea here. Must have been another leak from Madam's chamber did that."

Tanaquil stayed in the kitchen until the toast and fat was ready. She ate an orange while she waited, and watched Pillow's child trying to break her doll on an oven, but the doll survived and only went *Mamaa*!

Armed with the food, Tanaquil hurried back to the stairs to her room, and put the slimy toast out in the embrasure for the peeve. She had left her shutters ajar all night, but it had not returned. Somewhere it must have its burrow, lined with things it had rooted out or stolen. But she did not know where. And where had the bone come from? Somewhere in the sand, in the hot daytime—

It had occurred to Tanaquil that maybe the peeve's bone was an ordinary bone, only transformed by the magic overspill of the fortress. And yet, it had not looked, or *seemed*, of that order. The changes here tended to be ridiculous or alarming. The bone was only exquisite.

Tanaquil sat at her work table, fiddling with fossils, cleaning her repairer's tools, one of which had coiled itself up like a snail and needed to be straightened. Then she merely sat, with her chin on her hands, staring at the open window.

The peeve did not come back. She had annoyed or upset it. Perhaps it had bitten the bone in half and devoured it—surely that could not happen.

The sun turned hotter and bathed the room in light. The fat smelled, and a golden fly danced on it and feasted.

It was midday. The peeve had not and would not come.

Tanaquil stood up. She had found her divided skirt, and now tucked its hems into her boots. She swung into the window embrasure and out, and dropped the foot or so onto the sloping roof below.

Out here the sun was scaldingly hot. It was a world of roof hills and drainage gulleys, bushed with crops of weathervanes and old mysterious pipes. The copper roof slates greenly seared, and here and there were copses of chimneys. Above rose the tallest towers and the hedge of the battlements, where two soldiers passed each other with a bleary clack of spears. Was the burrow among the roofs, or had the peeve just decided to run up to her window on a whim?

Tanaquil picked her way along the copper slates, in and out of the shadow of chimney pots. The peeve might even have made a lair in one of the most disused of the chimneys. She peered into crevices, and found red flowers growing from cracks. Further over, under the eave of the library, was a large untidy nest once used by some ravens. They had caught speech and flown away yelling that the fort rubbish heap was not interesting enough. The nest lay in the shadow of a tower, and was protected by juts and slopes of the building.

Tanaquil lowered herself into a dry canal between the roofs and pushed through the flowers. At the canal's end was a cistern full of scummy water—it caught the snow by night and fermented by day. There were black paw marks on the cistern's edge.

To reach the library roof Tanaquil had to jump a narrow gap, through which she saw the kitchen yard below. Pillow and another girl, maybe Sausage, were hanging up some washing. They were small as the child's doll. Tanaquil took a breath and jumped. She landed on the library and heard Pillow say, far below, "Just listen, those ravens must be back."

One of the soldiers looked over from the battlements, too. Tanaquil had a moment's fear he might take her for an invader and fire at her, but he only waved.

The ravens' nest was empty, but beyond it a channel went back under the walls of the tower and the overhanging roof. Tanaquil moved on into deep shade, and stumbled over a pile of rugs and straw. The enclosure smelled of peeve, clean fur and meat and secrets. And there was a hoard of silly things—a small pan from the kitchen, some sequins, probably from one of Jaive's gowns, a spear-head . . . and, gleaming like white water in the shadow—"Seven," said Tanaquil aloud, "seven of them." Seven bones like the bone she had seen the previous night: two very little, and one very long, broken, and curved, like a rib, perhaps, and four exactly the same as the first, of which it must be a replica. And all of them like milk-crystal and stars.

"*Bad.*"

Tanaquil started guiltily. She looked round, and up on the ravens' nest the peeve poised in silhouette against the bright sky. Its fur stood on end, its ears pointed, its tail was a brush. Under its forepaws was another of the amazing bones. The eighth.

"In *my* place," said the peeve.

Tanaquil wondered if it would attack her.

Then its fur lay flat and its ears flopped. Its face took on a forlorn and sorry expression.

"Oh look, I'm not stealing from you," said Tanaquil, remorseful. "I waited for you to come back and show me the bone again. And when you didn't, I came here."

"My *place.*"

"Yes, to your place. Haven't you got a lot of these bones? Aren't you clever."

The peeve sat down in the nest and scratched behind its ear.

"Itch," it explained. It seemed to have perked up at her compliment. "Clever," it repeated.

"Of course they belong to *you*. But won't you let me help you find them—I mean, if there are . . . more?"

"More. Lots."

A cold shiver oozed down Tanaquil's spine in the boiling day.

"Will you show me? Can I help you?"

The peeve put its head down and studied the eighth bone it had brought. There was a silence.

Tanaquil said, "You know, the ravens might come back to their nest and steal from you."

The peeve tossed up its head and scanned the sky, its whiskers making fierce arcs.

Tanaquil felt like a villain.

"Let me help," she said. She went over to the peeve and gently stroked its head. The peeve allowed this and looked at her out of topaz eyes. "You are so *clever*. It's a wonderful bone."

They went out in the afternoon, when the worst of the heat was lessening. The peeve had been running back and forth all morning, only pausing to drink from the cistern in the roof gulley.

After all, the peeve seemed pleased to have company. It bustled along, sometimes rushing ahead, then playing in the sand until Tanaquil caught up. The direction in which they went was that of the rock hills. Tanaquil accepted this with an odd feeling in her stomach. When the little afternoon shadow of the hills came over them, and the peeve bounded in under the hollow hill shaped like a bridge, Tanaquil nodded. The hoard of fabulous bones lay exactly beneath the spot where she had brooded. Perhaps the dust storm a week ago had uncovered them, or even other playful peeves.

The dark heat under the arch of the hill was solemn and purple. Over among the tendons of the rock, the peeve excavated, sending up sprays of sand.

Tanaquil went to see.

And there, sticking up like crystal plants, were the tops of bones.

They dug together.

"Good, good," said the peeve, thrusting in its nose, and suddenly uprooting—there could be no doubt—a whole ribcage.

It was large, daunting. How it shone in the shadow. "Sprr," said
the peeve. They pulled out the cage of ribs, and leg bones
followed and dropped apart in jewelry bits. It was like the leg of
a huge dog, or like a horse's leg.

"Is there a skull?" asked Tanaquil.

The peeve took no notice, only went on digging. It had
apparently realized that, with Tanaquil to carry the bones, it
could unearth all of them.

They had worked in the hollow hill for maybe an hour when
the sand gave way, pouring down and over itself into a big
cauldron. Some of the bones just coming visible were folded
away into the sand-slip.

The peeve rolled about, kicking. Tanaquil used one of the
oaths the soldiers were fond of.

Very likely, the bones lay over a void in the sand; they might
tumble down into some hidden abyss, unreachable. The sand
might also give way entirely under Tanaquil and the peeve, cast-
ing them after.

Tanaquil tried to make the peeve understand this, but it paid
no attention, only resumed its digging. Tanaquil shrugged, and
threw in her lot with it, bracing herself, if she felt any movement
under her, to grab the animal and run.

No more slips occurred, and gradually the new bones came
clear again. There were parts of vertebrae, and the segments of a
long neck: star flowers.

Then, against her plucking hands, Tanaquil felt a smooth
mass. She heaved the object out. The sand shook off.

"No good," said the peeve. "Not a bone."

"It's the *skull*," said Tanaquil.

She held the skull in her hands, astonished, even after what
she had seen.

   It was a horse skull, or very like one, and it gleamed like
an opal, polished finer than the other bones. Colors ran through
the crystal of it, fiery, limpid. She imagined the brain inside this
case, which must have fed on such colors, or caused them. The
teeth were all present, silvery white. A pad of bone rose on the
skull, above the sockets of the eyes—layers of opal—indented
like another socket to hold some precious gem.

Tanaquil looked about. She was surrounded by the bones.
The peeve was still industriously digging, shooting sand into the
air, disappearing slowly down a hole.

"I think that's all," said Tanaquil. "Almost all of it's here."

"More," said the peeve.

"Let's go back now."

The peeve kicked and the sand gave. The peeve fell only a foot, but Tanaquil leaned down and took hold of it. It came out pummelling the air, sneezing angrily.

"Want dig."

"No, that's enough."

"Dig, dig."

"Let's take these bones to my room. They'll be safe there. You can share my room. You'd like that. I'll get you some lovely meat fat."

The peeve considered. It sat down and washed itself, leaving the bone hole be.

Tanaquil began to gather up the bones. She took the scarf off her head and folded bones into it, and put bones into the cuffs of her boots, into pockets. The ribcage was difficult; she somehow got it on to her back. She picked up the opal skull, cradling it in her free arm. "You take those." She indicated the last few slender vertebrae she had not managed to stow. The peeve got them into its mouth. Its mouth stood open, glittering.

Suppose someone saw them? Generally, the fortress might as well have been deserted during the afternoon. The soldiers and servants dozed, and Jaive swirled about her Sorcerium impervious to heat. Tanaquil hoped they would keep to their usual schedule; she did not want to share her discovery. Although she could not leave the fort, she had found a temporary escape—for the bones of the magical beast made her forget herself. In comparison to them, what did anything else matter?

The blast of the sunlight beyond the hill was mighty, but the sun was lowering itself westward and the sky was thick and golden.

Tanaquil and the peeve walked toward the fortress with great shadows before them.

Tanaquil told the peeve about the fat toast, and roast meat, and other things she thought she might be able to get for it. It kept pace with her, not arguing, mouth full of magic.

The peeve made a lair under Tanaquil's bed. It bundled up her rug and pushed that under, and took a pillow. Streams of feather stuffing eddied out from the torn pillow, across the floor.

As she arranged the bones along the floor at the opposite end of the room, she heard the peeve snuffling and complaining to itself, fidgeting about. It had eaten the rancid fat in the window, and she had brought some fresh from the kitchen, where only two of the sweeper boys were lying asleep on a cool stone oven. Now and then the peeve would emerge and watch Tanaquil's actions with the bones. "Please don't move them," said Tanaquil. It came to her that it would be better to suspend the skeleton in the air, from a ceiling beam, and she opened her work box, measuring lengths of fine brass chain, cutting these, and finding clips whereby to attach them—she did not want to pierce any of the bones, was not sure she could.

On the floor, the skeleton emerged into its true shape.

Tanaquil straightened up at last to stare at it.

Fragments were chipped, and there were gaps, missing pieces of the long spine, omissions in the ribcage—and below the right foreleg the small sharp toe of the hoof was absent. She could replace all the losses in less beautiful but adequate materials, so that at least the beast of bone was whole.

Without doubt, now she could see it was the skeleton of an extraordinary horse—but a horse also of extreme fineness, longer than was usual in the back and legs, the tail and neck, with the head also longer, and on it the strange pad of bone above the eyes . . .

The skeleton sparkled. It looked almost friendly. And then, by some shift of the sunset light, it altered, and a vague terror touched Tanaquil, like nothing she had felt before. Her mother did not believe in religion or priests, but Tanaquil wondered if she should make some offering to God. For only the God could know what this thing had been.

The light melted; the sun had set. In the deep blue sky the stars began to arrive, and the cold of night breathed at the window.

"You'll be warm here," said Tanaquil to the peeve. It snored in its lair.

Tanaquil climbed on her work table and began to put bronze hooks into the beam above—

The door was knocked. The voice of Bird, one of the girls who still sometimes absentmindedly cleaned the chambers of the fortress, came through its timbers. "Lady Tanaquil?" Tanaquil did not think she had heard Bird's voice for two months, had not met her anywhere. And now she was not glad to hear or see Bird.

"Just a minute!"

Tanaquil ran to the bed, swept off the topmost quilt, and flung it over the skeleton. Then she opened the door. Bird bowed, as the kitchen people, who saw Tanaquil most days, never did.

"Your lady mother sent me to fetch you."

"What does she want?"

"She's got a demon sitting in her circle of wax. I screamed when I saw it."

"She's always having demons in her circle. Why does she want me?"

"She just said fetch you at once."

"It's not convenient—" Tanaquil checked. If she did not go to her mother, Jaive might come sweeping down to find her. A visit from Jaive was rare, but then, so was a summons. "All right," said Tanaquil, and she came out, shutting the door. Bird had not seemed to notice the quilt, nor even the snow of stuffing from the pillow and smears of meat fat.

They went up the stone stairs. A wooden fruit detached itself from the banister and bounced away; neither girl reacted. The open landings were chilly, and outside braziers burned along the wall walks and the soldiers were singing sea chanties.

"Do you seek Jaive?" asked the jade head on the Sorcerium door.

"Oh, who else?"

"Your name and rank?"

But the door found itself being opened from within in mid-question, and looked insulted.

Bird gave a tweet and darted back down the stairs.

Jaive's chamber of magic was shrouded at the walls by a curious veiledness, like mist in a forest. The center of the room was clear, and there in the wax circle, lit by the burning tapers, sat a demon with two heads, elephant ears and frog eyes, a huge stomach, and no legs, for it stopped at the pelvis—or perhaps the rest of it was in some other dimension under the floor.

Jaive stood imperiously by. She observed her daughter, shook back her scarlet maze of hair, and said, "What have you been up to, Tanaquil?"

"Nothing," said Tanaquil. "How do you mean?" she added, more casually.

"Epbal Enrax says to me that weird elements have entered my fortress."

Epbal Enrax was the demon. It was called up about once a month. Tanaquil nodded politely. "How are you, Epbal Enrax?" The demon breathed out a mauve puff, which was a sign of contentment. "I don't see why," said Tanaquil, "you should think any weird elements here have anything to do with me."

"Epbal Enrax," said Jaive, "speak!"

Epbal Enrax spoke. The chamber shook, and pestles and parchments plummeted from cabinets—its voice was not loud, only *reverberant.*

"*Below,*" said Epbal Enrax, "*close by.*"

"Which is you, Tanaquil."

"It's also half your soldiers, the maids—"

"Continue, Epbal Enrax."

"*Red of hair sets fingers to a spark of fire.*"

Tanaquil shivered. Luckily the demon brought extra coldness—some of the taper flames had frozen—she had an excuse. She looked at her mother scathingly, and said, "He means *you*, mother. Red hair and sparks and all that. There's some stray spell of yours loose on a landing again. He's trying to catch you out. You told me demons are always prone to do that."

Jaive frowned, and turned to the demon.

"Here's my daughter. What of her?"

Epbal Enrax said: "*Rebellion.*"

Tanaquil had an uneasy feeling it was now assisting her deception. Demons would always cause mischief if they could. But she took the cue.

"Yes," she said, "it's that row we had, mother. About my leaving here. And you won't let me."

Jaive lost her powerful look. She was exasperated.

"Do you think I want to hear this nonsense now?"

"You fetched me here."

"What were you doing?" asked Jaive, with a last quiver of suspicion.

"What do I ever do? Mending something, fiddling about. I'm bored. It's infuriating. I want to leave and—"

"Be quiet!" stormed Jaive. She turned on the demon again and cast a bolt of light at him. The demon sizzled and began to whine. "You also be quiet! I'm surrounded by fools. If it's excitement you want, Tanaquil, we shall have a dinner in the hall. Yes, a feast, a party. You may wear one of your best dresses."

"That *will* be fun," said Tanaquil.

"Now go away. As for you—"

Tanaquil shut the door quickly, hearing the demon's cries and apologies all the way down the first flight of steps.

The fortress was in near-blackness now, an occasional lamp

left alight over the staircases and at the turnings of corridors, stars in windows, and brazier flicker.

Tanaquil opened her door and hesitated.

Through the darkness and through the cover of the quilt, a faint soft glow floated upward from the floor. The starry bones shone like the stars. Fingers to the spark of fire—had the demon really meant herself and what she did? What *did* she do? What sorcery beyond her grasp might she be unleashing?

She went into her room and stood shut in the night of it.

"Peeve," she called softly, "what are we up to?"

No answer. Tanaquil said, "There's to be a dinner. I'll get you a gorgeous meat bone—" and saw that the shutter had been nudged wide at the window. In the feathers on the floor were the marks of fat-sticky paws. The peeve was gone. Drawn by darkness, it had returned to the hollow hill in the desert.

Tanaquil felt a pang of anxiety. She was responsible for the peeve. They shared this adventure. No, that was silly. Who could control a peeve?

She lit her lamp and the glow of the skeleton faded.

"I'll just get on," she said aloud.

She thought of the sand giving way in the hollow hill and the peeve disappearing. Grimly, she got up on her work table and started once more to arrange the hooks.

How slowly the night passed.

Had she ever had a sleepless night before? Tanaquil could not remember one. Dissatisfaction and boredom had *made* her sleep. Now she was not bored at all, but alert, eager, very worried.

She had done all she could with the tools at her disposal. Tomorrow she would seek the blacksmith, who was one of the soldiers, hoping he was not too drunk to get the forge going. To her specifications he should be able to create for her those parts she needed to repair the beast of bone. A wild idea had come to her, too. Cogs and wheels, hinges and tiny shafts of bronze and copper might be incorporated into the skeleton, its legs, neck and spine. Perhaps it would be possible to make it move, to trot and leap, paw the ground, shake its head and twitch its slender tail. If she was canny, the blacksmith would only think she was at work on another, more complex, clock.

When she had done all she could, the night had swum out into the black hours of early morning. The moon had come and gone. The snow had fallen and frozen. Still shivering, Tanaquil had set a fire on her hearth and lit it.

She left the shutters ajar. Sometimes they creaked and she looked up—but the peeve was not there.

In the morning she would go and look, along the roofs, in the hill. Hopeless to try now; the cold would be impassable. She could not even find her wool jacket or cloak.

Finally, in the dull firelight, she put another quilt over the skeleton to hide its mysterious glow, doused her lamp, and went to bed.

She lay and looked at the normal glow of the fire on the ceiling.

Then she was out in the desert, hurrying over the rimy snow towards the fortress, and from above she heard the shouts of the soldiers, and they fired their crossbows at her but missed. Tanaquil half woke then, and heard the soldiers in reality clattering about and calling. But that was not so novel. They were always seeing things that did not exist and shooting at them. She picked up a dim cry: "It's only ghost-light on the snow, you idiot!"

Then she was asleep, and standing on the hollow hill like a bridge. On the western horizon the moon, which had sunk, was rising again. She watched it, and then she opened her eyes.

Some more time had passed. The fire was out. The room should have been in darkness, but it was filled with light. The moon had come in at the window.

And then Tanaquil saw the peeve standing on the foot of her bed. It was almost the scene of the previous night, except that she had left the way open for it. Except that now it held in its mouth a thing too large to have been carried with ease, long, and whorled like a great shell from the ocean, spiralled to a point thinner than a needle. And it shone, this thing, it *flamed*, turning the whole room, the peeve, Tanaquil, the air itself, to silver.

Then the peeve dropped its burden gently on the bed, and the vast light diminished, until it resembled only the starlight of the beast of bones. And so Tanaquil saw properly that what the peeve had brought her, from the sand under the hill, was a horn. And never having seen such a horn, she knew it, as would anyone who ever lived in the world.

"Oh, peeve," said Tanaquil. "By the God. It's a unicorn."

3

When Tanaquil opened her eyes five days later, the first thing she saw was not the painting of Jaive. Instinctively, Tanaquil had turned in her sleep, and lay facing her work table. And there above, hanging in space, spangling the sunshine from the window, was the finished skeleton of the unicorn.

It was eerie and beautiful, less like bones than some fey musical instrument. The replacement discs and tubes of burnished copper did not spoil it; they were only sunny patches of warmth against the crystal, and the hoof was a dot of fire. The skull of the unicorn was like a pale rainbow, and the horn, which by daylight seemed only a giant shell made of pearl, had been attached to the forehead with pins of bronze; a coronet.

The unicorn stirred faintly in an early morning breeze. The chains that held it from the beam were a bright rain. It was a sort of exquisite mobile.

In the joints of it were the thin shining levers and the wheels Tanaquil had fastened there at midnight.

Under the skeleton, on the table, sat the peeve.

The soldiers had remarked on the peeve, which had followed Tanaquil on each excursion to the blacksmith's forge. They thought the peeve was a pet. They admired its loyalty as it sat staring at the smithing work. Tanaquil knew the peeve was only interested in the parts for the unicorn. As she labored over it in her room, the peeve had watched her from its lair under the bed, sometimes coming out to paddle across her tools and upset them. It rarely spoke. Yesterday the herders had come to the fort, and large cuts of meat were now being prepared for Jaive's dinner. Tanaquil had brought the peeve several samples, which it had dragged under the bed to eat; a nasty, smelly arrangement that Tanaquil tried to overlook.

"Hallo, peeve," said Tanaquil now, letting it know she could see. The peeve ignored her. It slowly raised one paw, and before she could protest, it tapped the lowest bone of the left hind leg.

A sweet chiming note came from the leg, and echoed away through the skeleton.

Tanaquil sat up. The peeve jumped off the table backwards and shot under the bed.

"You see," said Tanaquil sternly, leaning down to confront the peeve's astonished pointed face, "I *told* you not to touch."

She got out of the bed and went to the suspended skeleton. Light as dust, she flicked at the bones of the forelegs, and other chimes winged over the room. She ran her fingers along the cage of ribs, and there was a rill like silver beads falling down a stair of marble.

She had not been able, last midnight, to bring herself to try if the unicorn would move. She was half afraid it might, and that movement would dislodge some bit of it, which would then come down and break. But also, she was just afraid.

The chimes of the bones filled her with awe. She stepped away. And going to the bed she sat there and only gazed at the skeleton, while the peeve put its head out and gazed too, saucer-eyed.

Bird knocked on the door, bowed, and held out a wave of olive-green silk.

Tanaquil's "best" dresses never went sorcerously missing, for her mother stored them in a closet of her own apartment. Tanaquil accepted the dress, a unity of floor-length, wide, rustling skirt, boned bodice, high neck, and complicated sleeves. It had a sky-blue embroidery of lyres and lilies all over it.

Bird spied past Tanaquil unavoidably.

"Ooh, what's that?"

"What exactly?"

"That dangly glittery thing."

"Just something I found somewhere. It's been there ages."

Bird looked doubtful, but she only said, "Your lady mother says I'm to attend you to the feast."

Tanaquil frowned. As she had feared, her mother was set on making the dinner excessive and full of fussy rituals. "I'm to wear my gray velvet gown," said Bird.

"Oh, *good,*" said Tanaquil.

"The gong will be struck just after sunset. Then we're to go down."

Bird was obviously looking forward to the dinner. Perhaps everyone was, except Tanaquil, who felt annoyed and almost embarrassed, for Jaive had suggested the dinner to Tanaquil as the cook had suggested she bake a cake.

When Bird had been persuaded to go, Tanaquil shut her door and tossed the splendid dress onto her bed, where the peeve came to investigate it.

Tanaquil was dissatisfied. She had found she did not want to go near her work table under the beautiful bones.

"This evening," she said to the peeve, "before the stupid feast, I'll see if I can't get it to move."

Then she turned her back on the unicorn skeleton and went to sit in the window. But it seemed to throw a far reflection on the desert, which glittered.

An hour before sunset, Bird came back to tong Tanaquil's hair into corkscrew curls. Something had happened to the tongs on the way. They wriggled and heaved and eventually got out of Bird's hands and strode on their two legs into a corner. The peeve hissed and spat at them from its nest in Tanaquil's dress.

"You shouldn't have let your pet get fur on your gown," said Bird.

They threw water on the fire they had meant to use for the tongs, and hoisted the peeve off the dress—"No, *nice*," it cried, clawing out lengths of embroidery—Bird dressed Tanaquil and exclaimed over her glory.

"I can't breath for these bones," said Tanaquil.

Everything was bones. The tight bodice, the peeve's stinky snacks under her bed, the glimmer of the skeleton from the beam—at which, now, Bird did not even glance.

The peeve sulked on the pillows.

"Go and put on your velvet," Tanaquil told Bird. "I'll meet you by the gong at sunset."

When Bird had gone again, Tanaquil knotted up the skirt of her gown and climbed on the work table. "*Now.*" Taking up one of the fine tools she kept for the insides of clocks, Tanaquil inserted it carefully into a small bronze screw. Next, using the handle of the tool, she hit the wheel in the foreleg of the beast. The wheel span, became a blur. A hinge shifted, a shaft narrowed as a pin slid backward—

"So you won't do it," said Tanaquil to the unicorn, boldly.
"You're meant to paw the ground—the air, if you like. Why
won't you?" She tried the same procedure on the right forelimb.
The wheel spun, the joints of bronze moved, but nothing happened. "Have I miscalculated the weight?" Less nervously, now
that she was disappointed and puzzled, Tanaquil tried to wake
the tapering tail, the brilliant head. There was no response.

Gradually the immobile unicorn of bone began to change to
ruby. The sun was setting in the window.

"If you won't, you won't."

Tanaquil got off the table. She knew a shameful relief, and at
the same moment she was drained, as if she had walked for miles
under the midday sun.

The unicorn swayed like a fire.

"I'll have to go down."

"Down," said the peeve. It burrowed under a quilt.

Tanaquil left the room and closed the door. Her hands were
full of pins and needles. Then she heard the gong booming
below, early, and gritting her teeth, descended to Jaive's dinner.

Jaive rose to her feet in an explosion of sequins. "We salute
the savory junket!"

Everyone else clambered up. "The savory junket!"

They all sat down again.

And the two old stewards, a pair of many called from
retirement in attics and cellars of the fort for such meals, hobbled
round the hall with their silver basins. On every enamel plate
they dolloped out the junket, which was sallow, and wobbled.

Despite the three lit fireplaces, racks of torches in demon-
shaped sconces, and the rose silk curtains along the walls, Jaive's
hall was always draughty. A solitary banquet table stood isolated
in the midst of it, facing an enormous round window of emerald
and red glass. Outside on this window, new patterns of frost had
already formed, ferns and fossil-like things. Beyond it lay the
darkening, freezing desert, its rough sand a mere five feet below
the glass—but the glass was sorcerous and only another sorcery
could breach it. From the carved beams, however, hung ordinary
cobwebs. There were holes in the curtains, and in the damask
table-cloth. The rats had parties in the hall when Jaive did not.

The painted doors at the south end of the room groaned
open for the fourth time.

Jaive rose.

"We salute the soup!"

Everyone else got up. "The soup!"

Everyone sat down.

Jaive sat at the table's center, in a tall ebony chair inlaid with sorcerous symbols of obscure meaning. Her guests had taken their usual positions. Tanaquil was on her mother's right hand; Bird was just behind her, with the other attending maids, Yeefa and Prune. On Jaive's left sat the captain of the soldiers in his dress suit of gilded mail and some battle honors that were possibly real. Down the rest of the table, left and right, were placed the captain's second-in-command and seven elderly retainers of the fortress, including Tanaquil's former nurse. Everyone had on their best, in some instances smelling of mothballs.

"We salute the baked fish!"

There was no fish ever to be had at the fortress, as it was more than a hundred miles from the sea. Instead the cook made a fish of salty pastry and painted it green with limes. It was borne in by a lame female steward of ninety years. The fish was always her task, and Tanaquil always expected the old lady would drop the plate, but somehow she never did.

Served, Tanaquil glowered at the doughy greenish lump before her, while around her the maids and the retainers chattered, and the captain and his second passed two of the wine flagons back and forth between them.

"A magnificent meal, Ma'am," Tanaquil heard the captain murmur to Jaive.

Tanaquil looked sidelong at her mother's face. Jaive wore the sublime expression most common to her. Her mind was always on higher things, the mountaintops of magic. Nothing could compare with those heights, but she conducted the silly dinner with a vague air of generously pleasing everyone.

The doors groaned.

"We salute the fruit ice!"

"The fruit ice!"

The ice was orange, and each scoop had an orange flower perched on it. The flowers neither changed into lizards nor flew away. Where her mother was present, the respectful spells stayed under restraint.

Tanaquil ate her ice. The cold of it entered her stomach like six cold words: *Those bones are nothing to me.* And then eleven more: *Nothing has happened. Nothing has altered. I shall never be free.*

The silver spoons lay in the empty ice dishes. Jaive spoke. "And now I will make an offering."

The retainers, maids, and soldiers became ponderously quiet, and the stewards straightened as they leant on their sticks.

Although not religious, at her dinners Jaive the sorceress always performed some worshipful act.

She left the table and walked into the space before the darkened window. She poured a stream of wine on the ground and cast some powder. The wine and powder mingled, fizzed, and bloomed up like a crimson rose. "We thank you for your gifts, and ask that you will share our feast, all benign powers. Let us in our lives humbly remember the perfect world, that is not this one."

The rose evaporated with a sweet perfume. Dazzling wisps trailed off into the ceiling.

The doors groaned.

"We salute the meat!"

"The meat!"

In marched two of the sweeper boys in clean white clothes, playing pipes and perhaps a tune. Behind them stepped Pillow and Sausage, strewing strips of golden paper. After the scullery girls stalked the cook, amazing in a cloth-of-gold apron, and holding in one hand a golden basting spoon, in the other an ivory flyswatter.

Following the cook came three black-and-fawn goats, washed and combed, led by the third white-clad sweeper, and drawing a small chariot on which rested the salver of the meat.

Tanaquil stifled a sigh.

The group of big roasts had been built into a towered fortress, with battlements of fried bread, roofs of crackling, windows of glazed red and yellow vegetables, embedded in dunes of mince.

There was greedy applause.

I might as well take the skeleton down, Tanaquil thought. *Put all those gleaming sticks, that rainbow skull, into a chest. A unicorn. I ought to give it to HER.*

Slices of meat were being served her by a steward of eighty-three. Another, of eighty-six, came up with a spouted golden vessel of gravy. Tanaquil thanked them. She thought: *I shall be here in this place until I'm eighty, as well. Or ninety.*

From somewhere, high up in her cranium, or higher, in the fort of Jaive, came a violent crash. Like a door thrust off its hinges.

A few faces were raised from forkfuls of roast dinner. Prune said, "There goes another of Madam's spells."

The captain said daringly to Jaive, "Better than the cannon, Madam." And Jaive smiled.

No more attention was given to the crash than this.

Tanaquil thought: *Perhaps an enemy has approached and is bombarding us! Some hopes.*

But there was still a feeling in her head, tingling and disturbing. It was like a white bright thought prancing down the levels of her brain, tossing its neck, with hoofs that slithered and struck sparks, landed and clicked forward like knives over a shield.

"Drink up your wine, Tanaquil," said her mother, "It will be good for your headache."

Tanaquil realized she had put her fingers to her forehead. "Mother, something's running down the stairs."

"Really? Just some little drip of magic."

"No, Mother, I think—"

Some obstacle tore open, some barricade of distance or sound. The thing in Tanaquil's mind seemed to leap out of it, and, loud as a trumpet from beyond the hall doors, came a brazen squeal of machinery run amok.

Prune, Yeefa, and Pillow screamed. The nurse, the old stewardess, and the goats of the meat chariot gave quavering bleats. The cook turned to face the doors, her spoon and swat at the ready. The captain and his second were on their feet, wavering slightly, but with drawn swords.

"Fear nothing, Madam."

Jaive was bland. "It will be a demon," she said. "I shall deal with it firmly."

Then the doors shuddered as if they had been rammed. They burst open.

What galloped through was a whirlwind of lights. It seemed to have no substance, only motion and prismatic flame. Colors danced off from it, blindingly. There were no chimes now. But there was the unmistakable whirr of wheels, the sharp striking of hoofs. More fearsome than the soldiers' swords, a savage horn slashed the air in pieces.

The skeleton of the unicorn. After all, it had begun to move. It had erupted into movement with a kind of luminous rage. It had snapped chains, knocked away doors, vaulted stairways.

It rushed along the hall, and Prune, Yeefa, Bird, Pillow, and Sausage jumped from its path squeaking. The boys yelled, the retainers doddered, the cook fell over in a bundle, the soldiers bellowed, jabbed and—missed.

Tanaquil had an impression of long streaks of lightning. In their center were tiny bronze whirlings. She saw a shake of the rainbow skull, and the soldiers flung themselves behind the wine flagons.

Jaive had got up from her chair. She called out some incomprehensible mantra and lifted her arms like sequined wings. Rings of power rolled out of her, but the unicorn was too swift. Nothing could catch it, stop it, slow it down. It leapt upon the table—plates and goblets were hurled away. The gravy in the meat dishes splattered up. Prune, Yeefa, Bird, Pillow, and Sausage rushed howling up the hall; the boys, the nurse and one or two others crawled under the tablecloth. The meat steward threw his stick, which smote the captain on the nose.

"Spirit of air or water, clockwork of fire or earth, take heed of the universal commandment!" declaimed Jaive.

The unicorn of bone splashed through her plate, and there, on the sequins of the sorceress, and in her scarlet hair, glowed gravy drops like sneers.

"It's me that it wants," said Tanaquil. She braced herself for the pain of the perfect horn breaking her heart. There was no margin for fright; she was not afraid.

But the racing framework of the unicorn dived by her. She dropped back into her seat astounded.

"*Stop, I say!*" shouted Jaive. Her face was flushing. She had had to come down from the heights, and she was angry.

Tanaquil watched her mother lose control in a marvelous fascination. Had *she* ever been able to make this happen?

The unicorn of bone pelted round the hall. It ran right to left, somehow sprang over itself and ran left to right, like the mechanism of a clock gone mad.

The goats kicked and butted and upset the meat salver. Everyone huddled at the core of the wild circlings. The captain, his purple sash to his bleeding nose, made rushes without leaving the table. "May the God help us," prayed the nurse complainingly from below.

Jaive clenched her ringed fists. Her body seemed to grow taller and to expand like a storm cloud.

"I call upon the force of iron to bind, of heat to consume—"

Tanaquil saw, across the turmoil of the hall, the peeve sitting in the open doorway. Its fur was all on end, its tail like a chimney brush. Like Jaive, it had made itself twice its proper size.

Tanaquil laughed.

There was a ripping noise. One of the silk curtains had caught the wild horn. The silk tore for several feet and fell down. The unicorn of bone was swathed in rosy silk.

"Do as I tell you!" screeched Jaive. *"Obey me!"*

And she flung some gout, some boulder of her magic, across the hall, at the unpredictable flying bone and silken thing that was chaos.

The air quaked.

"Oh the God," said the cook on the floor, "she's done something now."

Then everyone was silent. Probably they did not even breathe. The big, echoing draughty hall was abruptly choked, *filled,* as if stopped time had been stacked there. No one could move. Tanaquil thought she felt her heartbeat, but miles away beneath her feet. She turned her head, and it went with difficulty, as if she were submerged in thick glue.

And how gluey dark it was. The torches and the fires had changed to a horrible black-red.

Across the length of the room strewn with quivering girls, broken crockery, gravy, and goats, Tanaquil saw the heap of torn curtain brought down where the flying thing had been. Jaive's boulder had hit it. Now the curtain had no shape. No smart of hoofs, scud of wheels, no cosmic gleam and glitter.

"Mother, what have you done?"

But Tanaquil's voice did not leave her mouth, because the glue was also in her throat.

As for Jaive, she had shrunk back, not to her natural dominant size, but somehow smaller. Her hair, in the gloom, was without any color.

And then a spear of pure light lanced across the hall.

Tanaquil gasped. It was as if strings were fastened in her heart, and now someone pulled on them.

The heap of torn silk bubbled; it erected itself like a tent, then suddenly slid over. Something rose up, and the silk ran off from it.

Jaive's hall was now filled by the light of a snow moon.

And in the light, which was of its own making, the radiance of its seashell horn, Tanaquil beheld the unicorn.

The unicorn.

It was no longer only a beast of bone. It had grown flesh and form. It was black as night, black as every night of the world together, and it shone as the night shines with a comet. On this burning blackness, the mane and the flaunting tail of it were like an acid, golden-silver fire off the sea, and it was bearded in this sea-fire-acid, and spikes of it were on the slender fetlocks. Its eyes were red as metal in a forge. It was not simply beauty and strength, it was terror. It rose up and up to a height that was more, it seemed, than the room could hold, and its black shadow curved over it, far less black than itself.

Jaive said, quite steadily, "I greet you. But by the powers I can summon, be careful of me."

And the unicorn snorted, and a fiery gas came out of its nostrils. It scraped the floor with its forehoof, and there was a rocking in the hall, like a mild, threatening earth tremor.

And then the unicorn leapt up into the air. It was like an arc of wind, and passed with a sound of far-off roaring, bells, thunder.

Where it came down, beyond the dinner guests, the mess, and the table, it struck the round sorcerous window with the horn. The window gave like a plate of ice. Fragments sheered off to hit the sky and the cold of the night and the snow blew in. But the unicorn blew out. It soared into the pit of empty darkness and was gone.

Then Tanaquil knew what tugged on her. She knew because it pulled her up and forward in a ridiculous scramble. Before she understood what she did, before anyone could think to grip her, she had bolted over the hall, into the hole of the window, and jumped down onto the snow-crusted sand. She felt the freezing through her silk shoes as she ran, and dimly wished she had not worn them. But really she did not grasp what had happened. The sky was colossal, and the land too. And the unicorn raced. And faintly at her heels she heard the fur barrel of the peeve thump down after her, and the skitter of its paws pursuing her, as she chased the unicorn into the desert waste.

PART
Two

4

She was very cold.

Perhaps she should get up and light the fire.

Tanaquil opened her eyes. She was already on her feet, and her room had grown much too large. It had no furniture. There was a carpet of white snow, walls and high ceiling of pale black moonlit night.

A sheet of horror fell down and enveloped her.

She knew what had happened, what she had done. Of course, she had been enchanted or possessed—her meddling with the bones had seen to that. In thrall to the unicorn she had chased after it, in a mad trance. Now, coming to, she found herself on the face of the desert, and, turning slowly round, saw nothing anywhere that was familiar, but only the snow and the sand and the night, which were everywhere the same. Her mother's fortress was not in view. The rock hills were out of sight.

Something gleamed in the moonlight on the snow, coming down from a rise. It was a track created by the narrow hoof-marks of the unicorn. Each had filled with ice and curious green-ness. Each shone like a pock of stained glass from Jaive's shattered window. The other way the track led on across the snow into the distance. She must not follow this track. She must retrace the steps the way they had come. Her own footfalls had left no imprint.

Tanaquil walked quickly along the glassy trail. She went up the rise. This must have taken a quarter of an hour. At the top she looked over and saw the snow and sand stretching to the edge of vision, nothing on it, no clue. And the weird trail of the unicorn had vanished. Some night wind had blown over and erased it.

Had she really come all this way? She could not remember

it. It was as if she had been asleep, yet in the midst of an exultant dream, like those she had had before of running across the snow.

Well, there were no doubts now. She had emerged from the ensorcellment and would freeze to death in a matter of hours.

"No," said Tanaquil aloud. There would be rescue. Jaive would send the soldiers after her. They would catch up to her soon, she had only to wait.

Miles off, a jackal gave a wail at the moon.

Tanaquil listened. Sound carried vast distances. Yet she could hear nothing of any soldiers. But then, they would have to come from the fort, they would be erratic and fuddled . . . could they find her? Probably Jaive would put the magic mirror into service. But again, there were no landmarks here. Even if Jaive gained a glimpse of her daughter, could she be sure where she was exactly?

Tanaquil was now too cold to shudder. Her feet and hands were numb. She jumped up and down and beat her palms together.

As she was doing this, she saw something bounding toward her.

Was it a starving dog or antisocial jackal?

Dressed for the dinner, she did not even have her knife. She must use her fists, then.

"Hey!" shrilled the dog or jackal. It was neither.

"Peeve—"

"Rock," said the peeve, flinging itself against her legs, "big rock with hole."

"Do you mean the hills?"

"Rock," said the peeve. It took a mouthful of her dress and pulled on her. Tanaquil gave up and ran with it. They hurried over the snow, sometimes slipping or falling. The night had become one large ache of cold and blundering.

The rock seemed to appear from nowhere, looming up out of the dunes. Tanaquil had never seen it before. It was the size of a room and had a low doorway, a cave that pierced into it. Tanaquil and the peeve crowded in. It was a shelter, but felt no warmer than the open ground outside. In a shaft of the westering moonlight, Tanaquil began to see tufts and skeins of thorny plants growing inside the rock. The forlorn idea came that, if she had had her tinderbox, she could have made a fire.

The peeve would survive in the desert, it was a desert animal. Unless it had forgotten how, from living at the fortress.

When she sat down facing the cave entrance, the peeve got into her lap. They pressed close for warmth.

"If my mother's soldiers don't find me . . ." said Tanaquil. She felt exhausted. She would drop asleep, and might not wake up again. She talked on determinedly. "But they will. What a fool I was."

"Gravy," said the peeve, apparently for no reason. It slept.

"How did you know about the bones?" asked Tanaquil. "The unicorn must have ensorcelled you, too. Must have drawn you there to dig them out. And I repaired it. And Jaive's magic bolt brought it back to life. And . . ."

If I don't freeze, and live till morning, thought Tanaquil, *I shall be fried alive by the sun.*

No, they'll find me in the morning, or I'll find my way to the fort.

In the cave entrance the moonlit ice shimmered.

A bright shadow came picking over it.

Tanaquil clutched the sleeping peeve. She watched, rigid, as the unicorn came down across the white dunes, over the silence, to the mouth of the cave. There it lowered its fearful head, and its eyes like coals flamed in at her.

Perhaps it will kill me. Then I won't have to wait to freeze or burn.

Tanaquil's teeth chattered.

The unicorn raised its head. Now she could only see its body, the hard slim greyhound curve of its belly and the long and slender legs. It pawed the stone floor just inside the cave. A shower of silver sparks littered through the air, and came in at the entry. They clustered on one of the dry thorny bushes growing in the floor. For a moment the bush seemed full of silver insects. And then curls of smoke were creeping from it. The bush was alight.

"Oh!" Tanaquil rolled the peeve from her lap. On her knees in the low cave she crawled about, breaking off the twigs of the bushes to feed the blaze.

Like something taking flight, the unicorn lifted away. It vanished, and only the moon shone on the snow, and the hot fire on the floor of the cave.

Tanaquil dozed through the night by the miraculous fire, attentive so it should not go out. She fed in the sticks sparingly, and the peeve lay luxuriously on a fold of her dress, stomach exposed to the warmth.

Nothing else came near for the remainder of the night, and she might have accused herself of dreaming the unicorn, but for the fire.

When the sky began to lighten, Tanaquil went out of the cave and scraped rime and snow off the top of the dunes, putting the sandy stuff in her mouth. She was not yet thirsty, but once the sun came she soon would be. The peeve did as she did, licking busily and congratulating itself.

Tanaquil tore off a third of her embroidered skirt, leaving the bright blue petticoat to protect her legs. She fashioned a head covering from the skirt, and bound her hands with strips of the material. She cursed her shoes.

The peeve became excitable as the sun rose. It bounded about the cave entrance. "Going? Going?"

"Yes. We'll go and see if we can't meet someone."

The sky was a pale and innocent blue as they set off. It was pleasant at first after the harsh night. But they had to walk with the sun. Tanaquil kept her head down.

The going was hard over the sand, as always.

They went on for about an hour. Gradually the comforting heat of the sand changed. It started to bake and blister. Each step was a punishment. The gong of the sun blared in Tanaquil's eyes and beat just above her head.

Tanaquil thought ferociously of ice. Mountains of ice, scorching her with cold. They melted.

Another hour passed.

Tanaquil wanted only to lie on the sand. Eventually she had to sit down. There was no shade or cover in any direction. She could hardly swallow.

"Mother," croaked Tanaquil, "what are you doing?"

The thought came that Jaive imagined Tanaquil had rejected her. After all, Tanaquil had threatened to leave. Perhaps Jaive believed Tanaquil and the unicorn were accomplices. In that case, would Jaive renounce Tanaquil? Would Jaive abandon Tanaquil to the desert?

Tanaquil bit her lips. She wanted to cry, but shedding tears would only make her thirst much worse.

Suddenly the peeve went flying off. Tanaquil croaked at it; it took no notice, disappearing over the slope of some dunes to the left. Had the peeve also abandoned her?

"She could have sent one of her demons," whispered Tanaquil from her husk of throat. "She *could* have found me. She's a *sorceress.*"

One tear came out of her right eye. She would have pushed it back if she could. Why should she cry at her mother's neglect? Her mother had always neglected her. Tanaquil was a disappointment to Jaive, who had obviously wanted her daughter to be exactly like herself. They had nothing to say to one another.

"Confound her," gasped Tanaquil. "That's that."

The sun was very high; time had moved quickly as she sat there in a stupor, and it would soon be midday. Tanaquil began to scoop the scalding sand aside, making a burrow for herself. It was not deep enough, but she got into it and curled up, scrabbling back the sand. She felt as if she were being cooked, but the direct rays of the sun were now lessened. She doubled the skirt to protect her head and face.

I'll survive. Something will happen.

She tried not to hope the unicorn would return. But she dreamed or hallucinated that it did so, and struck the sand with its horn, whereupon a stream welled out. Instead, it was the peeve licking her forehead and cheeks with a hot, sandy tongue.

Tanaquil attempted to embrace the peeve, but it insisted on thrusting something against her mouth. Tanaquil recoiled. The something was a snake the peeve had hunted and killed over the dunes.

"Meal," said the peeve.

Tanaquil looked at the snake dubiously. It had been attractive before the peeve attacked it. Now it was a broken piece of raw meat she did not want. However, it would be sensible to eat some of it, and ungrateful not to.

"Thank you."

"Welcome," said the peeve. It commenced eating the other end, showing Tanaquil how good the snake was by making noises and screwing up its eyes.

Tanaquil managed to extract, chew and swallow some of the snake. The flesh was cool, soothing her throat. But the fine skin upset her. Mirages swam before her eyes, gardens, and lakes with boats on them, such as Jaive had shown her in the mirror. She thought how Jaive always harped on about how badly made the world was, and that there were others even worse, and one created perfectly. Evidently Tanaquil's world was all wrong, a place where you could only live by murdering other creatures.

Every animal preyed on another. Even those who got by through eating herbage destroyed the living fruits and seeds. In the perfect world there was a perfect food which all there ate. It was not alive, did not have to be attacked or slaughtered.

"Just look, there's the sea," said Tanaquil to the peeve.

She lay down on the sand with the green cloth over her face. She was aware of a faint extra shade. She realized the peeve had sat by her head, and the sun as it turned from the zenith began to cast the shadow of the peeve's body onto her.

Tanaquil thought Jaive was combing her hair. She was rough with the comb, and Tanaquil protested. They were in a boat on a lake. The boat bobbed violently, and Tanaquil was slammed up and down against the cushions. The peeve landed on her chest. It looked up past her head, snarling at Jaive, who was still raking Tanaquil's hair with the comb.

"Ow. Mother, please," said Tanaquil.

She raised her heavy gritty lids, and the sun lashed at her eyes. Something was pulling her by the hair. She was bouncing over the dunes, and the peeve was scrambling about on her, spitting and hiccuping in wrath.

Tanaquil squinted. Without surprise, she saw the night-black shape, the day-flame of the horn pointing exactly over her.

The unicorn dragged her by the hair.

This was a dream.

"What are you?" said Tanaquil to the unicorn. "I mean really what are you? Where do you come from? What do you want?"

She was hauled up a hill of sand, behind which the sun flickered away. And then the sun burst out again, and she was tumbling and cascading through a river of grains and particles, the dusts of the desert's centuries. Choking and coughing, she plummeted twenty-five feet into a hard gray bruise. The peeve revolved past her and fetched up, head down, in a sand drift. From this it emerged without dignity and in great noise.

Tanaquil smiled. Although the bruise she had hit had duly bruised her, she now lay in a long blue bar of shade that seemed cold and lovely as a river.

For some while she let it console her. Then she watched the sun, divided by a tree, making gold among great fans.

Then she rolled over. The bruise was a stone, marking a vertical tunnel in the sand. It was a well-head, with a well beneath. The well had a leather bucket. It had deep, cold, black water in it.

The blue bar of shade stretched from a single palm tree of impressive height. The peeve, recovered, had already climbed the trunk and was bumping about in the coppery leaves. A shower of dates pattered into Tanaquil's lap.

The peace of the oasis was wonderful. It gave no warning that night must return, the well freeze, and the snow come down. At the oasis afternoon stretched out forever.

Tanaquil was not thinking at all. She had given it up. Everything was nonsensical anyway.

The sun swung lower, and the sky congealed in darker light. The shadow of the palm seemed to go on for a mile.

Tanaquil looked along the shadow and saw another mirage. This time it was of a jogging movement of the land. The sand went up in a burnished cloud. Forms like beasts began to appear out of the cloud, and riders and carts. The mirage was not like the others. It had a sound, too, a rumble and mutter and the clean singing of small bells.

Tanaquil watched the mirage benignly. It came closer and clearer, and grew louder. Tanaquil saw five cream camels, with colored tassels and men up on their hilly backs, swaying forward out of the dust, and then the big wheels of three carts with six mules walking before each one. She saw men in tunics, trousers, and boots, with cloth swathing their heads, and next three more camels of brick red, with rocking silk cages perched on their tops.

She got up. She would have to start thinking again.

"Peeve, listen to me. It's a caravan—it truly is. Of course, this is an oasis. They may be—must be—going to the city. Now, we have to be clever. No mention of my mother—they very sensibly won't trust sorcery. And peeve—don't *talk*."

"What talk?" said the peeve. It was part of the way up the palm trunk again, staring at the approaching caravan.

Tanaquil stood, dizzy and stunned, never having known before such elation. For these were strangers—people—and they were going to a city.

"Good evening, girl," called out the man with the goad walking beside the first cream camel. "What are you selling?"

Tanaquil blinked. "Nothing."

It occurred to her that persons from villages might gather at an oasis where a caravan was due, in order to offer produce to the travelers.

"Then why are you loitering here?"

Tanaquil was affronted. "I'm here to join your caravan. You're going to the city, presumably?"

The man glanced up at the three riders on the nearest camels. All four men laughed. It was not proper laughter, but more of a sort of threat.

"Yes, we're going to the Sea City. You'll have to ask the caravan leader if you can join us. We don't take any old riffraff, you know. There's the fee, as well. Can you pay it?"

Tanaquil had not thought of this. She spurred her brain. Just as it was no use boasting of a sorceress mother, so it was no use expecting strangers to offer her care.

"I'm from the village of Um," said Tanaquil.

"Never heard of it."

"Few have. It's a very small village. I saved up to buy a place in a caravan, but as I was coming here I was set on and robbed. They took everything, my money, my donkey. I almost never got here. Now I'm afraid I'll have to throw myself on your kindness."

The men regarded her. She was only really used to the soldiers, drunk most of the time, and easygoing, who actually had treated Tanaquil more like a wise elder sister. Now Tanaquil saw how most of the men of the world looked at most females. It irritated her, but she concealed this. She smiled humbly up at them. There was a code in the desert, she knew. You could not leave the lost or needy to perish.

"All right," said the man on the ground, striking the goad against his boot, which was hung with small silver discs. "You'd better see the leader." He turned and raised his arm, calling loudly back into the dust and trample of the arriving caravan: "Night's rest! All stop here!"

The caravan sprawled about the oasis in the sunset. In all, there were seven covered carts, and these had been drawn up to make a wall against the desert. In the gap between each pair of carts burned a fire. Jackals had approached, and howled to each other in the near distance. The palm tree and the well were the center of the camp. Here water was drawn continuously, and dates—and incidentally the peeve—had been shaken down.

"What's that?" the man with the goad said, pointing at the peeve. "Funny-looking thing."

"My animal," said Tanaquil.

The peeve growled, and Tanaquil tapped its head. "Ssh."

"*Bad*," said the peeve.

"Eh?" said the man with the goad, glaring at the peeve.

"Oh," said Tanaquil, "it's just barking."

The man with the goad was called Gork. His head cloth was secured by a silver band, his dark clothes were sprinkled with ornaments, and across his chest hung a large gold pocket watch. He constantly ticked and clinked, and when he felt he was not making enough noise, he rapped the goad on his boots and whistled.

"This way. The leader's awning is going up over there."

Under his awning, the leader of the caravan sat on a chair in the sand. He had been journeying in one of the silken cages on top of one of the three pinkish camels that had brought up the rear. He was a fat man with a beard.

Gork explained the situation in his special manner. "This bit of a girl's come after us, but let herself get robbed on the way. She hasn't a penny, and expects us to take her on."

"I'm afraid we couldn't do that," said the leader, not bothering to look at either of them, only into a box of candied grapes. "You must pay your way. Food alone is expensive, not to mention our protection."

"You can't," said Tanaquil firmly, "leave me in the desert to die."

"Well of course that would, technically, be against the law," said the leader. He beamed upon the grapes. He said nothing else.

The peeve stirred restively at Tanaquil's side.

Tanaquil said quickly, "My three brothers at Um know I meant to join this caravan. Eventually, if they don't get word from me from the city, they might seek out the caravan's leader."

"She's a nuisance, isn't she?" said the leader to Gork. "Give her that lame mule on Wobbol's cart. And a snack to tide her over. Then she can bundle back to her village."

"I don't want to go back to Um," said Tanaquil. She clawed at her wits and said, "Isn't there something I can do to earn a passage with you?"

"What on earth *could* you do?" asked the leader, looking at her for the first time, as if she were a rotten grape found in the candy box.

There was a spluttering crash and chorus of yells and oaths.
Up on the dunes, the watching jackals cackled.

The leader, Gork, Tanaquil, and the peeve all turned to see.
Displayed in the firelight, one of the carts had thrown a wheel.
The cart now listed, and the man who had been at the wheels,
cleaning them of sand and oiling them, lay feebly struggling
under several large bags and sacks that had fallen out. Men ran to
rescue him—or the bags and sacks.

"Useless," said the leader. He ate another grape. "Deprive
that fellow of rations tomorrow."

"Trouble is, leader," said Gork, beating on his boot, "Wobbol
was the only one who was any good at repairing wheels and stuff.
And as you remember, Wobbol went off in a huff when you
bought his cart and load off him at quarter price—"

"Yes, yes," said the leader. "The goods will have to be put
onto the mules."

"The mules won't be able to take it, leader, not for all those
miles."

Tanaquil felt light-headed. What had happened to her was
crazy, but also it must have been right. For now everything
conspired to help her. Surely she would never see the unicorn
again, and she would come to disbelieve in it, with time. But still
a kind of magic was working about her, because she had taken
the risk.

"Don't worry," she said, "I can fix your wheel."

"You?" said Gork.

The leader only grimaced; he had sly, flat eyes.

"Don't mock, Gork. Let's see if she can. *If* she can," he
added, "she can travel with us, eat with us, no charge. On the
other hand, if she *can't*, I'll throw her to those jackals."

Tanaquil shrugged. It was on her tongue to say the jackals
would be preferable company anyway to the leader, but she did
not. Instead she walked over to the spilled cart, the bristling
peeve on her heels.

"Clear these sacks out of the way," said Tanaquil, in the
imperious tones of her mother. "Are there any tools?"

Presently she was kneeling by the cart. Since it *was* Wobbol's,
she suspected he had engineered the faulty wheel out of revenge.
The wheel shaft was set crooked, and the pin in the wheel had
snapped. Tanaquil organized one of the fires into a forge. She
sent the caravan servants running about to fetch and carry. Herself, she hammered out the new pin from a brooch she was

handed. It did not take great strength. Even Gork came to watch the stupid village female who could mend wheels.

When the wheel was soundly back in place, Tanaquil stood up.

"That's a fair job," said Gork grudgingly. "Where'd a girl learn that?"

"My brothers taught me," said Tanaquil prudently, "at Um."

5

For almost three weeks Tanaquil traveled in the caravan. Every hour she was excited. Every hour she lived with a sense of insecurity and danger she had never known before. She was out in the world.

At least once a day, they would pass some marker in the sand, indicating the route to the city. Most of these were plain stone posts about ten or eleven feet in height, often looking much shorter where the sand had washed against them. But as they came nearer to the city, there began to be occasional stone pylons stretched up at the sky, carved with prayers or quotations. On the ninth day they reached another waterhole. On the sixteenth day, near sunset, there was a large oasis of palms, acacias, and fig trees, with a village at its edge. Tanaquil was nervous; they might put her off here. Nothing else had had to be mended, and she added weight to the cart in which she traveled. The peeve, too, had caused problems. Although she had still been able to convince listeners that its grumblings and exclamations were an odd type of barking, she had seen various people, including the merchants who rode in the silk cages, making superstitious signs against the peeve. Twice it had gone among these merchants' shelters at night and used someone's costly rug as a bathroom. The previous night had been the worst. The peeve had laid its dung near the head of sleeping Gork, then, in covering it, nearly buried the man alive. However, no sooner were they in the oasis, than frowning Gork's gold pocket watch ceased ticking. Having shaken it, cursed it, and hurled it in the sand, Gork found Tanaquil at his elbow. He gave her the watch with awful threats, but she repaired it in half an hour. Not even a hint was made after this that Tanaquil should leave the caravan.

The leader she seldom saw. He rode by day as the merchants

did, in a bulb of silk pulled over a wicker frame, on a camel. The other men in charge of the caravan gave orders, shouted, laid down the law on every topic, discussed chariot races, and played violent gambling games. The male servants treated Tanaquil much as one of themselves, although she was a girl and therefore inferior. She had been given their castoffs to replace her gaudy dress. As far as she could tell from splits in the sacks, smells, and accidents, the caravan carried cakes of soap, sugar, conifer incense, and paper, from a city to the east. Tanaquil had never heard of this city. Her mother, who had given her lessons, had only ever spoken of the city to the west. Was this significant?

Mostly Tanaquil tried not to think of her mother at all.

Also, she tried not to think of the unicorn.

The unicorn was something so bizarre that it could only happen once. If that. Perhaps it had assisted her in the desert, or perhaps she had only made that up. Maybe the bush had caught alight in the cold cave naturally. Maybe she had only crawled by herself towards the well.

It seemed to her now that it was possible she and the peeve had not found anything under the rock hill. That nothing had gone wrong at Jaive's feast except that Tanaquil herself had flung open a door and run away.

One morning she actually said to the peeve, "Do you recall the starry bone you found?"

"Bone?" said the peeve gladly, "where?"

And a merchant going by, fanning himself, glared at the peeve and made the sign against evil spirits.

It was the nineteenth day of Tanaquil's journey with the caravan, and a wonderful sunset inflamed the sky, glowing vermilion and amber, with clouds in the west like furled magenta wings. The general opinion was that they would reach the city the following evening. Everyone was pleased, and the servants had all day given Tanaquil tales of the city that were plainly quite absurd. The city's prince was supposed, for example, to have a palace of white marble fifteen stories high. Tanaquil nodded politely.

In the afternoon they had passed a great obelisk with a brass arrow at its top pointing west. The prayer on the obelisk read: *We give thanks to God, who brings us to Sea City.*

The desert changed. Low rocky cliffs drew up out of the dunes, and then the cliffs had dry brown shrubs on them, and

here and there a warped, wild tree. As the light blushed, they
came into round hills with stands of green cedar. Flocks were
pastured, and little villages lay in every direction, one after another, with their fires and lamps burning up like bits of the red
sky.

The leader came down from his cage and mounted a mule.
He rode at the head of the caravan, with Gork walking beside
him. "We'll spend the night at Horn Spring," said the leader in a
ritualistic, syrupy voice.

Tanaquil felt something like a twitch of a curtain inside her
mind.

She turned to one of the servants, Foot.

"Why is it called Horn Spring?"

"A sacred legend of the city," said Foot.

"An ignorant villager like me," said Tanaquil, "hasn't heard
of it."

"No," sneered Foot. He decided to be nice to her. "They
say a prince from the city came there. It was a very sandy year,
and he was parched with thirst. He asked the God for water, and
a beast with a horn ran up out of the desert and cleft a rock with
this horn, and out burst the water."

"How convenient," said Tanaquil. The hair had risen on her
scalp.

"Watch it, your funny animal's in the soap again," said
Foot.

The sky was wine-red, fading. The caravan wound up a
dusty trail and they were on a bare dark hill. Above, the top of
the hill ended in a big rock, like a chimney. Under the rock was a
grove of trees and another well with a stone curb, which was not
spectacular. The leader got off his mule and, going to the well,
thanked God for the caravan's safe arrival.

The camp was made below the grove, and water drawn from
the well. Foot advised Tanaquil to drink some, as it was very
health-giving and said to grant wishes. Tanaquil, though, did not
go to look at the well; it was dark now, and growing cold, the
thin snow whipping out on a buffeting wind that rose soon after
the sun set.

Tanaquil sat near one of the fires and ate her rations, sharing
them with the peeve. "What shall we do in Sea City?" she said to
it, then hastily, "Don't say anything, here's Gork."

"Nasty," said the peeve.

"That animal really does have an odd bark," said Gork. The

peeve snarled and went under a cart with a salted biscuit. "What will you do in the city?" Gork asked Tanaquil with unknowing repetition.

"Oh, this and that."

Gork studied his pocket watch, tapped his boots and whistled. Next he said quietly, "Are you courting?"

Tanaquil was amazed. Should she be flattered or laugh? Very seriously she replied, "I'm afraid I am. My brothers betrothed me to someone in the city."

"Those brothers don't seem to look after you properly," said Gork.

"But they're my menfolk, so I have to do as they say."

"Yes, quite right."

The peeve bit down on the biscuit with a cracking noise, and Gork straightened and whistled up at the snow. Without another word he went off. Presumably, thought Tanaquil, he had seen the value of a lady love who could mend his cart wheels and his watch.

And then the sound began.

She took it for some purer note of the night wind, at first. It seemed everywhere around, ebbing and flowing.

She thought, idly, still accustomed to the supernatural things of Jaive's fort, *Perhaps there are demons on the wind.*

"*Aaeeh! Look! Look!*"

A pot dropped and smashed. To the eerie sweetness of the wind's tone was added the din of panic. Three servants, who had been descending from the well, had stuck in their tracks, letting fall water jars and wailing, pointing away above the grove of trees.

The whole camp was suddenly in confusion. Men drew knives and cudgels. The merchants emerged from their awnings with whinnying cries, and one sank to his knees, reminding God he wanted protection. The camels, too, were stamping at their pickets, roaring and snorting, while the mules brayed maddeningly.

"A fiend! a *monster!*"

"*Kill* it!"

"*Run!*"

Tanaquil stared over the hill, up along the chimney of rock. She got to her feet as if raised by cords.

Atop the chimney was a blackness on the night blacker than the night. It seemed to have no form, yet there was a flicker over it like foamy fire. And out of it burned two crimson stars beneath a sword of light.

Slowly it turned, this sword, to east and west, south and north, catching on its spiralled ribs, its pitiless point, the blasting of the wind. And the wind played the sword, the wind made music. The sword of the horn *sang*, and now the camp, even the vocal camels and raucous mules, fell silent.

"You exist," said Tanaquil. And before she knew what she did—again—she held her hands out into the air, as if to touch that creature on the rock some fifty feet above her.

But with a splash of whiteness, of black, the unicorn had turned and bounded off into space. The music ended. And over the wind, Tanaquil heard the voice of the praying merchant.

"Just look at her, the witch. Can't be trusted. She calls up demons."

Tanaquil left the sky. All the men had moved up around her. They stood on the hill glaring at her. The knives and sticks made a forest, and for a moment she could see nothing else.

Then the fat leader pushed through. He observed her distastefully.

"I took you in, girl. I let you keep that animal, which my good patron Pudit said was bewitched. Don't trouble with her, I said. She means no harm."

"I don't," said Tanaquil.

"Then why did you conjure a demon on the rock?"

Tanaquil recalled her raised arms, and how it must have seemed.

"I didn't conjure it. And it wasn't a demon—" She almost blurted that she knew a demon when she saw one, and just stopped herself in time. "Don't you know what it was? It was a unicorn—"

The leader gave a sour laugh. "No such thing."

She thought: *He'll believe in something supernatural and evil, but not in the glamour of a unicorn.*

The merchant Pudit had approached. He said, "There's only one method with a witch. She must be stoned."

"Sounds reasonable to me," agreed the leader. Then he was yodelling, leaping up and down, and kicking in the air his left leg, which had a brown fur trouser.

Men rushed to his assistance. The peeve, detaching its teeth with an annoyed growl, sprang instead at the merchant Pudit. It bit him several times, while Pudit's servants, trying to strike the peeve with their bludgeons, thwacked the merchant on the arms and chest.

Tanaquil was not sure if the peeve had meant to create a diversion so she might escape. If so, it failed, for Foot and one of the others had grabbed her by the arms.

After a few more moments of incredible noise and flurry, the peeve in any case let go and fled. It dashed between legs and flailing sticks and vanished down the hill faster than a falling boulder.

"Bitten to the bone," announced the leader. "The animal's her familiar."

Tanaquil noticed there were plenty of stones on the hill, and some of the men had begun to pick them up.

She watched, stunned.

Then she saw Gork thrusting through the crowd, coming over and standing before his bitten leader, clicking and clinking and with the goad going *clock-clock-clock* on his boot.

"It's no good killing her," said Gork. "That'll be bad luck."

"Rubbish," said the bitten leader. But the men with the stones had hesitated.

"Now don't you remember last year?" asked Gork.

There was a long pause. Whatever had happened last year was obviously being remembered in detail.

"That was," said the leader, cuddling his leg, "a different thing altogether."

"Well I, for one," said Gork loudly, "won't travel with a caravan under a witch's dying curse. Nor my men. Eh, boys?"

There was a cluttering of dropped stones.

"All right," said the leader sullenly.

"We'll drive her out," said Gork. "Let her go and talk to demons in the hills." He was rewarded by hearty amalgamated assent. Gork said to Foot and the other man, "I wouldn't touch her if I were you. Who knows what the slut might do next." Then he came over and put his face near hers. Gork winked. He cried: "Be off, you filthy witch." And gave her a weightless shove.

Tanaquil nodded. She turned and ran down the hill, and the men moved back from her, a few shouting names. A thrown missile burst near her heel, but it was only a clod of earth.

As she ran she thought of the useful small knife and the tinder-box she had bartered away from Foot, in exchange for the torn silk of her dinner dress. She thought Gork had probably saved her life. And that the unicorn, which had saved her in the

desert, had somehow played a trick on her tonight, stirring up
from the peaceful dark danger and uncertainty.

Tanaquil sheltered that night in a cave of the hills, with as
much space as she could manage put between her and the caravan. Bushes shielded the cave mouth, and the fire she lit. Sometimes she would stab the fire with a branch and describe aloud the
leader, Pudit, Foot and certain others, in vivid terms. To her
muttering and firelight the peeve was guided in the early hours of
the morning. It had killed a small rodent, and this she apologeti-
cally roasted for them. The peeve seemed indifferent to its own
loyalty.

They fell asleep, and were woken by sunrise.

When she walked out of the cave, Tanaquil saw that the hills
slipped gently down westward to a great plain. Lit by the rising
sun, a golden crescent glittered on the plain's farthest edge, and in
the curve of it the sky had swum in on the land.

"It's the city," Tanaquil told the peeve. The peeve groomed
itself, not sparing a glance. "And beyond, there's the sea."

She was very impressed. She had a second of wanting to
jump up and down and shout, but she controlled it.

Very likely it would take some days to cross the plain, but
Tanaquil was reassured by the landscape as she descended into it.
The sand had given way to thin grass, in places to tracts of wild
red and purple flowers. Palms and acacias grew, and later there
were orchards of palm and fig, olive trees and lemon trees,
behind low walls. Villages lay along the plain like stepping stones
to the city. Tanaquil entered one boldly, and asked for fruit.
They took her for a boy with very long hair, gave her the fruit,
and were astonished at the "tame" peeve.

Tanaquil and the peeve walked all day, and Tanaquil had
words with her ill-fitting cast-off boots. At sunset the wind rose
eagerly. Men appeared in the orchards to cover the younger trees
against the cold. Since there was another village in front of her,
Tanaquil went into it and inquired of a woman on the street if she
might have shelter for the night. "I can mend things," Tanaquil
added, enticingly.

The woman gave her use of the barn, and presently the
village music box was brought her in pieces. Tanaquil sat on the
straw, bootless, working on the box, while the peeve chased real
and imaginary mice, and the thinnest snow painted in the rims of
the village. When she was finished, they gave her a supper of

peppery porridge and olives, and took the music box away. She heard it playing from house to house until midnight.

In the night, *night* passed down the street.

Waking, Tanaquil saw under the barn door four black stems with flags of lighted ocean. She heard the shell of the horn scrape along the door. She felt the terror of it, the magic, and the impossibility that it should be there or that she should go to it.

"What do you *want?*"

But the unicorn only moved through the village like the wind, silent, without music.

Just before dawn, four or five women were staring at pink glass hoof-pocks in the rime by the well.

"What's this?" they said.

"Oh, whatever can it be?" agreed Tanaquil.

The peeve laid seven slain mice, subject to the laws of the cruel, badly made world, at the feet of their hostess.

So Tanaquil, daughter of Jaive the sorceress, finally reached the city she had been vaguely hearing of for nearly sixteen years.

She felt so elated that day at having got there, it was almost as if she had invented and built the city herself.

First of all, coming out of some trees, Tanaquil found one of the stone obelisks. This marked the start of a paved road. It was quite a narrow road, however, and empty; looking to either side over the plain, Tanaquil could see in the distance evidence of much dust and traffic obviously going along wider roadways to the city.

The narrow road, which would have taken a light cart and mule, ambled through groves of lemon trees and lilacs, and in one place there was a stone basin with water and an iron cup connected to it by a chain. The chain settled for Tanaquil an idea that had been bothering her.

"Peeve, do you mind if I put you on a leash?"

The peeve had found a lemon and was trying to eat it. She peeled the lemon for it and, while it investigated the pith, Tanaquil tied 'round its neck the long sash that had secured her headcloth. The leash was rather clumsy, but it would serve for now, and might prevent comment from the city people.

The peeve spat out the lemon and clawed at its neck.

"No, no. I'm sorry, but you must put up with it."

"Off," said the peeve, "off! Off!"

"No. *Please.* Just till we get—wherever we're going."

"Wurr," said the peeve.

It rolled about and became entangled with the leash. Tanaquil patiently disentangled it before it strangled. "Half an hour?"

The peeve sulked as they walked along the road. Every so often it would sit down, and Tanaquil would find herself hauling it over the paving on its bottom. The peeve swore. It had learnt some of the soldiers' oaths.

"Or you can stay outside."

The city was surrounded by houses that had grown up under the wall. There were gardens with cypresses and banks of flowers, blue and white, yellow and mauve and red. The houses had roofs of dragon-colored tiles. The wall stood over them, and it had, as reported, tiled pictures on it of chariots drawn by racing horses, of lions, trees of fruit, and so on. The narrow road ended at a narrow gate, where two soldiers stood to perfect attention, like dolls.

Out of the city came an enormous noise. There seemed to be every sound on earth taking place at once. Tanaquil heard wheels rumbling, engines that toiled, buckets that rattled, and water that swilled; she detected cattle lowing and dogs barking, while trumpets crowed, doors slammed, birds flew, men and women quarrelled and laughed and sang. She was taken aback. *Well, what did you expect?*

The peeve was gazing at the city's noises in disbelief, attempting to snuff out all its smells, including that of the sea.

"Lots of bones and meat and biscuits here," said Tanaquil.

She sauntered toward the gateway, and all at once the two soldiers came alive.

They clashed over the entrance to the city their crossed spears.

"Halt."

Tanaquil halted. What now?

"State your business in Sea City."

"I'm visiting my aunt."

"You will produce her letter inviting you."

"I don't have it."

"Without such a letter or other confirmation, you can't enter the city."

"My aunt will be furious," said Tanaquil.

The soldiers did not seem distressed by this news. They said nothing, their faces were blank, and the spears remained locked.

"What are the grounds for entering?" said Tanaquil.

"An invitation in writing from a citizen. A summons by the Prince or other dignitary. The bringing of merchandise into the city. The desire to practice a legitimate business there. One word of warning," added the soldier. "*Don't* say you *mend things.* We hear that feeble excuse about twice a day."

"I see. I didn't understand." It seemed to her she had never made a plan so swiftly. "I'm an entertainer. I do magic tricks."

"This may be allowable. The bazaar supports entertainers. But you'll have to give proof."

"You mean you want to watch me perform? That's rather awkward. You see, I was robbed in the desert. They took everything——my donkey, my bag of tricks——"

"How can you carry on your business in the city then?"

"I do have one thing left," said Tanaquil. "You see this peeve? Just an ordinary desert creature. But by a clever illusion, I can make it appear to *talk.*"

The soldiers turned their mask-like faces on her.

Tanaquil abruptly tugged the peeve's lead.

The peeve kicked. It parted its jaws. "Rrr!" it went.

Tanaquil coughed. "Sorry. Dust in my throat. Try again——"

She toed the peeve quite mildly in the side.

It spat. "*Bad,*" said the peeve. "Won't. Don't like it. Go desert." And spinning in the sash it managed a short dash and pulled Tanaquil over. As she and the peeve tumbled on the hard paving, she heard the soldiers split their masks, giving off guffaws.

"That's a riot," one choked. "Can you do it again?"

"Once is enough for now," said Tanaquil.

"Bite!" cried the peeve, chomping on the sash. "Wup!"

"Yes, that's really terrific!"

The peeve swore, and the soldiers almost had a fit. They uncrossed their spears and clapped Tanaquil much too heartily on the back as she dragged the squalling peeve into the city. "Good luck, boy. That's a marvelous turn you've got there. We'll tell all the lads."

6

Every exaggerated fantasy Tanaquil had ever had of the city was outstripped by the facts. Even Jaive had never demonstrated, in the magic mirror, anything like this. It was like being inside an enormous clock of countless parts and pieces. It seemed at once jumbled and precise, random and ordained. Just like the sound it made, which was a mix of a thousand sounds, so its shape was formed out of all shapes imaginable—lines, angles, bumps, cones, rounds—and its basic colors of brown, yellow and white, were also fired by the noon sun into blooms of paint, fierce blinks of metal, and cracked indigo shadows.

Tanaquil did not try to take it in, she simply marched in to it, staring about her wildly, overwhelmed. While the peeve accompanied her in noisy bewilderment—the million scents of the city had entirely taken up its attention, it growled and whined, snuffled, grunted, and sometimes squeaked. Now and then it ran sideways after something or other, and Tanaquil, her concentration scattered, was tugged against the brickwork or into the mouths of lean alleyways. She thought of undoing the leash and allowing the peeve to rush off on its own. Perhaps she would never see it again—something dreadful might happen to it. It knew the desert and was as surprised here as she was.

At first, near the gate, there had been few people, only the small groups you might come on in a village, women in doorways or at a well, or some men going by with spades over their shoulders. Then the streets, winding into and around each other between the walls and under the arches, opened on a broad white avenue. Palm trees of great height grew along the avenue, and there were marble troughs of water, to one of which three polished-looking horses had been led to drink. The sides of the avenue swarmed with people of every description, and at the windows and doorways and on the balconies of the buildings along the road, were crowds thick as grapes on a bunch. Flights of steps went up too high to see, from the avenue, what was at the top, and up and down them strode and ran the citizens, sometimes colliding. Tree branches curled against the sky from gardens on rooftops. Stained-glass windows flashed as they were constantly pushed wide or closed. The road boomed with voices, and with the vehicles that went both ways along it, chariots and carts, silken boxes carried on the shoulders of trotting men, and one stately camel under a burden of green bananas.

Tanaquil stalked up the road, pushing through the human swarm as she had noted everybody else was doing. The peeve, on a very short leash, kept close to her now, its muttering lost in the general uproar.

Soon wonderful shops began to open in the buildings. She saw shelves of cakes like jewels and trays of jewels like flowers and sheaves of flowers like lances and, in an armorer's, lances like nothing but themselves.

She wanted to look at everything, to laugh and to shout. She felt taller than anyone in the crowd. Also she was dizzy. There was too much, and she was drunk on it, as the peeve had got sozzled on smells.

The end of the avenue was an even further astonishment. It expanded into a marketplace, a bazaar, where every single public activity known to the world seemed to go on.

Two pink marble lions guarded the entrance, and Tanaquil and the peeve rested against the plinth of one of these while porters, carts, and the banana camel trundled by.

Tanaquil attempted to view the things of the market individually, but it was impossible. Her eyes slid from the baskets of peaches to the bales of wool to the pen of curly sheep, to the juggler with his fire-work knives and the fortune-teller's tent with the wrong sorcerous signs embroidered over it, and on.

The market went downhill and was terraced to prevent everything tipping over. But Tanaquil's gaze tipped all the way down, and there below, in a rainbow frill of objects and actions, bluer than the sky, bluer than anything, was the sea. Contrasted to the flurry of the shore, slender ships glided slowly across the water, on russet and melon triangles of sail. The fishy, salty scent sparkled like glass in the air, stronger than perfume, sheep, and peaches.

"Oh, Mother," said Tanaquil, "we salute the *fish!*"

"Now then, move along for God's sake," said a beefy man in an apron. He shouldered past.

"Be good," said Tanaquil to the peeve, "and I'll—" she hesitated. She had been going to promise to get the peeve some cooked meat from one of the stalls. But of course, she had no money. Indeed, she had never *seen* money except in Jaive's coffer, and more recently at the dice games of the caravan. "Er, we'll see," said Tanaquil. They would not starve. She had, did she not, her fabulous magic "trick"? Instead of gawping at the bazaar, she should find a pitch and thrill the unsuspecting populace with the talking peeve.

They went into the market, and walked down the terraces through flares of blood-red silk and garlands of woven baskets.

The juggler was encouragingly earning a large pile of coins, tossed by the crowd. In another place a girl danced with bells on her wrists and ankles, and elsewhere boys made a living pyramid, and fire was eaten.

Tanaquil and the peeve came against a side of ox in which the peeve was rather interested. As she tried to separate them, Tanaquil beheld another marble lion ahead. Seated between its feet was a man playing a pipe. As he played, he swayed, and out of the wooden bowl before him rose a swaying snake, itself with a skin like a plait of bright money.

"Just look," said Tanaquil to the peeve, prizing it off the ox carcass. The peeve looked, for once obliging. Tanaquil realized she had made a mistake. "No—"

The leash burned through her fingers and was gone.

Like a flung brown snowball, the peeve demolished the distance between itself and the marble lion. The crowd about the statue's base parted with cries. The peeve skirled through. It rose steeply. It landed.

There was a kind of explosion of tails, paws, bowl, pipe, snake. Fur and scales sprayed up in the air.

The piper stood baying and waving his arms, obviously afraid to intervene in this cyclone. The unsympathetic crowd laughed and jeered.

An awful clattering rebounded on the marble. The snake was gone, instead, a heap of scales and wobbling springs lay on the lion's feet. The peeve, with a silver spine and head in its mouth, galloped at Tanaquil.

She caught it. *"Bad,"* said Tanaquil, inadequately. "You fool, it's not even real—"

The peeve crouched at her feet, worrying the silver backbone of the mechanical snake and growling. It seemed slightly embarrassed.

"I'm so sorry—" Tanaquil hurried to the statue and looked up at the snake charmer, who was picking over the shattered bits of his act.

"Seventy-five weights of copper and three pence this cost me," he moaned. "Made by the finest craftsmen in the city. Now see."

The peeve had followed Tanaquil, trailing its leash. "Give me *that*." She got the spine and head from its teeth, and it seemed glad to forget them in a thorough wash. The head had faceted green glass eyes, and hinged jaws of ivory fangs. Tanaquil began to try the springs back against their slots. "I think I can mend this."

"No, no, just my rotten luck. Ruined."

"Really, I think I can. I *can* mend things."

The snake-charmer glared at her with tearful eyes.

"*You're* an artisan?"

"Well—I suppose so."

"All right. *Do* it then."

"I'll need some tools—"

"An artisan and no tools," scoffed the embittered snake-charmer. He sat on the lion and refused to glance at Tanaquil, the peeve, the crowd, or the snake.

"Over there, Bindat's stall—he'll lend you a few artisan things," said a man who had come across from the meat rack. "Meanwhile, you can pay me for the bite your dog's taken out of my ox."

"I haven't a penny," said Tanaquil.

The man surprisingly answered, "Have it free then. It was worth it for the laugh."

All afternoon, Tanaquil sat under the marble lion and repaired the mechanical snake.

It was quite a difficult job, but the further she went with it the more she got the hang of what needed doing. The scales, which she had feared might be the worst task, merely linked into one another with tiny hooks.

As she worked, people stopped to watch. Ignoring the peeve tied to a post and the snake charmer lurking on the lion, a few inquired what Tanaquil would charge for mending a toy, a clock, a small watering device. Tanaquil said, "I charge half the going rate."

This meant that by the time the sun westered, various items had been left in her care. The bazaar did not shut up shop with sunset; already lamps and torches were being lit.

"Here you are," said Tanaquil raising the renewed snake in the reddening light. "See if it will go."

"Of course it won't. Hair-fine mechanisms—"

"Just *see*."

The snake charmer snatched the snake and cast it in the bowl as if he loathed it. But he blew a trill on the pipe. The snake stirred. To swaying melody, the snake flowed upward from the bowl and danced at the sunset.

The snake charmer took the pipe from his mouth, and the snake hovered upright, gleaming.

"I won't thank you. Your dog broke it in the first place."

"No, *please* don't thank me," said Tanaquil. "After all, it might become a nasty habit."

She flexed her fingers, swallowed her hunger and thirst, and, taking up the two halves of a doll soldier, began again to work.

Four hours later all the left items had been collected, and a pocketful of coins sat gleaming like the snake under the torches.

Somewhere a bell sounded. It was midnight. Looking up, Tanaquil found a ragged man in front of her. An iron cap was over his head and covered his eyes. He probed an invisible void with his stick. A blind beggar.

"Clink, clink," he said. "I heard the coins fall. Spare me a coin."

Tanaquil put a coin into his thin searching hand.

She remembered the unicorn with a shock of the heart. This imperfect world—

Bindat's wife, Cuckoo, suggested that for the payment of three pennies, Tanaquil might spend the night in their outhouse. Tanaquil was exhausted and accepted. They had a long walk, however, to Bindat's house, which lay behind the great market and far from the beautiful avenue, in an area of slums. Here the dwellings leaned on each other to stay up, and rickety wooden bridges went over the streets, and washing-lines, from which, even as they passed, thieves were stealing the washing. Bindat and Cuckoo even greeted one of these thieves warmly. They crunched through open drains, frozen by night, and came to Bindat's house. The outhouse was a hut with holes, white with frost.

Wood was stacked there, and it was busy with beetles. The peeve, leash off, spent all night chasing and eating these beetles, despite the bowl of thin soup it had shared with Tanaquil. In the morning, very early, Tanaquil learned that, in addition to the three pennies, she must pay for her lovely night by sweeping the yard and milking the goat. As a child, for a treat, she had sometimes milked the goats at her mother's fortress. This was harder, as the goat and the peeve had declared war on each other.

After a breakfast of burnt crusts, Tanaquil and the peeve returned with Bindat and Cuckoo through the hot and reeking drains, and lamenting owners of stolen washing, to the bazaar. Tanaquil was delighted to find a queue of people waiting for her under the marble lion: Word had got around.

At noon, Bindat came over to Tanaquil and told her in a friendly way that he would have half her earnings, as he and Cuckoo had personally sent all her customers to her. As he spoke, Cuckoo might be seen cleaning a large knife at their stall.

Tanaquil did not argue. She gave Bindat half her coins. When he was gone, she told her next customer she would be moving to the tents of the spice-sellers, whose smell had already attracted her.

Once she had returned all the previously mended things to their guardians, she slipped away, and descended the terraces out of Bindat's sight. Among the spice jars, at an obelisk with a stone fish on it, she sat down again with the peeve, and as she resumed her work, she watched the fish market below, and the blue sea that was greener against the harbor.

Once or twice during the night in the outhouse she had dozed. Then she had believed the unicorn poised outside the door, clean as black snow in the slum. But waking as the peeve scampered over her in its hunting, she knew the unicorn could not be there.

Now she felt she was working in a set of condiments—the pepper and ginger, cinnamon and hyssop and anise, with the fishy salt of the sea.

The peeve sneezed and ate the baked joint she had bought it. Then it slept on her foot after its hard night, and her foot also went to sleep.

A shadow fell across Tanaquil as she was fastening the frame of a mechanical board game involving a lot of small porcelain animals. She glanced up. Her new customers were three large men. The central figure wore black and red clothing, and the buckle of his belt was a gilded hammer crossed by a brass chisel.

He said ringingly, "I am Vush."

"Well done," said Tanaquil.

Around her, the chatter and frisk of the spicery had gone quiet. Everyone was staring at Vush and his two burly companions.

"You don't know me?" asked Vush. He had a terrible beard, which lurched at her as he spoke.

"I'm very sorry."

"I am the Master of the Artisans' Guild of Sea City."

Tanaquil received an inkling of alarm. She grabbed the peeve's leash at the neck. It was already practicing a snarl.

"How nice to meet you," said Tanaquil.

"It's a girl," said the companion to the left of Vush. He shifted, and Tanaquil saw his guild apron, and that he too had the hammer and chisel device, and a brass-bound cudgel.

"Then," said Vush, "she should be at home, not here causing trouble."

"Oh dear, have I?" Tanaquil groveled.

Of course it was apparent what had happened. She did not need Vush's right-hand companion to announce: "Bindat reported you to the guild. He says you charge half the going rate for your work. All prices are fixed by us."

"And you're not a member of the guild," said Vush. "Which means you're not allowed to work in the city at all."

"I didn't know," said Tanaquil. "You see, I come from this backward village—Um—and nobody ever said—"

"Give me that," said Vush, pointing at the game.

Tanaquil thought, *He's going to smash it. Perhaps over my head.*

Before she could make up her mind to let loose the peeve, Vush's left-hand crony leaned down and skimmed the game away.

Instead of hitting her with it, all three ponderously examined its mechanism.

"Not a bad bit of work," said Vush at last.

Tanaquil simpered. "*Thank* you."

"We have no women in the guild," said Vush. "You'll have to join as a boy."

"But you'll have to join," added the right-hand crony. "Or it's the harbor for you."

"You mean you'll put me in a boat?"

"We mean we'll drop you in the sea with lead sandals."

"I'll join," said Tanaquil. "An honor."

"The fee is forty weights of silver."

"Oh."

"You'll have to get someone to sponsor you, pay it for you. One of the guild members may do so."

"Then you'll be in his debt."

"You'll have to work extra hard to pay it off."

"You'll need the guild, then."

"Yes."

The peeve reached out and aimed its claws at Vush's expensive boot. They missed.

"Come to the Guild Hall at sunset," said Vush. "Anyone will direct you."

"If you don't come," said the left-hand man, "we'll come looking for *you*."

"Too kind," said Tanaquil.

She longed for one of Jaive's spells, which, according to Jaive, would have transformed Vush and Company into frogs.

It was true that everyone seemed to know where to find the Guild Hall of the Artisans, or at least the people Tanaquil asked directed her without hesitation. The building stood on another fine street, bathed in the sunset, and its gilded pillars shone, and the symbol of the hammer and chisel shone above the door. The door, though, was firmly shut. Tanaquil, with the peeve on a new strong leash bought that afternoon, knocked politely, and next violently, but without response. Perhaps the artisans' baleful invitation had been only a dare, or a joke to make her look foolish. This hope was destroyed when, from a round aperture above, a fat, frowning male face stuck out.

"Who is there?"

"I was summoned here by Vush the artisan."

"You're the woman from the market. Control that animal." The peeve was scratching at the gilt on the pillars.

As Tanaquil tried to control the peeve, a smaller door in the great door suddenly slid open. Tanaquil stepped through, pulling the peeve with her. The small door, a thing of clockwork, snapped shut again behind them.

They were in a long corridor lighted by hanging lamps. At the corridor's far end was a second massive door. The only option was to go forward, and this Tanaquil did. No sooner had she begun to walk toward the second door than mechanical

oddities activated all around her, perhaps triggered by her foot-falls on the floor. Bells chimed, tiny windows flapped open, and wooden birds whizzed out—the peeve leapt at them—plaster heads turned menacingly, poking out red plaster tongues. Tanaquil thought it all rather crude.

When she reached the door, the peeve struggling beside her, trying to make plain its needs—"*Bird! Bird!*"—Tanaquil knocked once more, and this door flew wide.

The Artisans' Hall—it was labelled in gold lettering on the wall facing the door, above another gold hammer and chisel, some gold saws, braces, measures, and other stuff—was exactly square, washed with black, and lit by torches. On black chairs around it sat thirty men whom Tanaquil took for officers or superiors of the guild. And facing the door, beneath the lettering, was a man who must be Vush, for his chair was the largest, and a fearsome beard escaped beneath the mask he wore. Every man in the room was masked. The masks were all the same, bronze visors with panes of black glass at the eyes. Meant to create a sinister impression of uninvolved ruthlessness, the masks had succeeded. Tanaquil wavered between scorn and extreme uneasiness. And catching her mood, the peeve crouched, speechless and bristling, at her feet.

A voice came abruptly from the air. Another device, but startling.

"Here is the boy Tanaquil. He is able to mend games and toys, and seeks admission to our guild. Meanwhile, he has worked without membership and owes the guild a fine of three weights of copper. Also he cannot pay the fee of membership. A sponsor is asked. Say brothers, will any do this service for the boy Tanaquil?"

One of the masked men, thin and bony, cranked to his feet. Sourly, he said, "Vush the Master has proposed that I do so. I'll therefore pay the silver for the boy Tanaquil, which he will then owe me as a debt, plus interest to me of one half-weight of bronze, all cash to be returned to me during the next year, before next year's Festival of the Blessing." He sat down.

"We heed," said the voice in the air, "the generosity of our brother, Jope. Does the boy Tanaquil hear and comprehend? Does he owe that he will honor this loan, and repay it at the proper time?"

Tanaquil shrugged. "If I must. If I *can*. Do I have a choice?"

"No," said the mask with Vush's beard. "Answer correctly."

"I'll repay the loan," said Tanaquil. "What if I can't?"

"You will be whipped through the city by the guild, as a defaulter," said Vush's mask, annoyed.

"Wait," said Tanaquil. "I'll give it up. I won't mend anything. I can find different work."

A loud murmur came from the room, and she picked out another of the masks saying, "I told you, it's that girl I heard of with the animal that talks."

Vush cleared his throat, and the hall was silenced.

He said, "Too late. It has been decided." And then he thundered: "Bring forth the Fish of Judgement."

With a slight rumble of hidden wheels, part of the floor moved sedately backwards, drawing twenty-nine of the chairs up to the walls, while Vush's chair ran in a graceful arc to the right.

The peeve growled.

The wall with the gold symbols and lettering split on a high rectangular door.

Tanaquil had a glimpse of trees in some yard or garden behind the Guild Hall, of peacock-blue evening sky sewn with stars—escape—but something came instead into the hall, and the door closed.

The voice in the air droned:

"From the sea comes the wealth of the city. To the sea we give homage. Let the sea be our judge."

An iron table was sliding from the wall and up to Tanaquil. On it rested a bronze balance, the two cups of which swung as it advanced. There was a strong, now-recognized, odor.

The brotherhood of the guild arose. "The Fish!"

Tanaquil thought of her mother's dinner.

In the left-hand cup of the balance lay a silver-scaled fish. It was artisan's work, and beautifully made, like the snake in the bazaar. In the other cup of the balance was another fish. This was greenish gray and smelled to high heaven. A real fish, from the fish market.

The guild brothers were raising their masked heads and arms.

Vush said, face to the ceiling, arms upheld, "Choose now, boy Tanaquil, which fish is it to be?"

Not having had the ceremony explained to her, Tanaquil assumed she was to choose the made fish, which anyway would be more pleasant. On the other hand, perhaps the reeking real fish represented honest toil? If she chose wrongly, what ridiculous and ghastly punishment would be inflicted?

She thought, irresistibly, *The last idiotic ceremony was my mother's dinner. The unicorn got me out of that.*

She pictured one of the doors that led into the hall crashing open and darkness flying in behind the seashell moon of the horn.

Then she looked down again at the two fish.

There was only one.

Was this divine intervention? The fish that was left was the nice example, which had been made.

"Well I suppose," said Tanaquil. She stopped because the artisans had also lowered their heads, and even through the masks she guessed they were gawking at the empty cup on the balance.

"Where's that fish?" said the sour voice of Jope.

"It was here," said another one. "I *smelled* it."

"Without the fish the ceremony is null—"

"Where, oh, where—?"

"*There's* the fish," tolled Vush.

Tanaquil became aware that something hot and furry sat by her leg, and from its pointed face, out of its motionless jaws, drooped three inches of silvery green tail.

Tanaquil snatched the made fish from the other cup.

"Behold!" cried Tanaquil. "I choose the fish that is made. But my peeve has chosen the fish which may be eaten."

"Sacrilege!" moaned Jope. "The ancient ritual has been mocked. Am I to put up all that fee for her now?"

"This is certainly very grave," said Vush.

Tanaquil confronted the ring of wicked-looking masks, the laughable dangerous darkness of these men, who were probably even madder than her mother, and much more unjust.

"What punishment for eating the fish?" moaned the wretched Jope.

"The fish," muttered Tanaquil, "the meat, the soup, the stairs, the door—I put you together out of bones and clockwork and you came alive—Is this a spell I'm making? Where *are* you?"

"She's seen our hall," said Vush, "and the ritual of membership. But she can't join. It would be bad luck on us all."

"It's the harbor for her," said a voice she recalled.

7

The wall under the letters, hammer, and chisel *changed*. Then, quite easily, it parted. There again were treetops and a darker, bluer sky of wilder stars. Pernickety as a cat, the unicorn came, as if on shoes of glass, in through the opening, down across the hall. There was no violence, no speed. It moved to the rhythm of an elder dance, putting all the rituals of the world to shame. Black, silver, gold, and moon-opal, night and sea, fire, earth, air, and water.

This time I did call it. Or every time I did.

At her feet Tanaquil heard the peeve swallowing the whole fish in one gulp. And the unmuffled drum of her own heart.

Then one of the artisans shrieked.

"It's the Sacred Beast! Fly! Save your lives! The city's lost!"

And somehow the mechanical chairs were knocked over, and the shut door to the corridor was wrenched open, and out of it the artisans sprang and sprawled with masked shouts and frightened thumps.

The unicorn, mild-mannered as a deer, trotted lightly after them. It went by Tanaquil like a wave of stars. She thought she heard the music of its bones and of a night wind wrapped about the horn.

As the unicorn passed through the door and along the corridor toward the outer exit, the peeve tugged on its lead to follow. And once more Tanaquil was propelled to chase the night-dream thing.

In the corridor the plaster heads turned and poked out their tongues irrelevantly, and then there was the street beyond the opened pillared door. And down the street rushed the artisans in their secret regalia, revealed, speechless now in the single-mindedness of panic. With the unicorn dancing after.

Tanaquil hauled on the leash. "No—let it go—I shouldn't have—no—no—" And the leash snapped and the peeve bounced out into the street, pursuing maybe only its old fantasy of a meal or a treasure—the bone—and Tanaquil *walked* after. She forced her mind to do some work, while her feet tried not to run.

How had the unicorn entered the city? She saw it leap from the sky like a falling planet. But no, the event had been more simple. She seemed to see the narrow gate through which she had come in, and one soldier asleep by a wine flask, and the other standing idle, regarding something come quietly up out of the groves and orchards of the plain. A horse? Yes, a fine horse lost by some noble. And the horse came to the gate, and the soldier who was not drunk enough to be asleep smiled on it, and tried to pet it, and somehow could not. But he undid the entry to the city, and like a vapor the unicorn went in. "Horse-horse," said the soldier fondly. "One day, I'll have a horse."

There were torches burning along the street at intervals, and here and there a lamp hung in a porch or a lit window gave its stained glass brilliance.

Through cold arches of shadow and cold blasts of light the fleeing artisans milled. They panted like rusty bellows now, and sometimes groaned or cursed. One or two craned over their shoulders, now and then, and, seeing the slender blackness of their terror still nimbly prancing after, made fresh rushes of flight that soon broke down.

Nobody looked out to see what went on. The city was full of noises day and night. They met with no one, either.

However, at its end, the street was crossed by another, a wide avenue of special splendor. It was lined by lions of gilded iron, and had lamp standards with lanterns of sapphire, green, and crimson glass. People were passing under these, and there was something of a crowd at the road's edges, standing and looking along the street with mild concern.

The artisans had no charity for this barrier. They plunged into it, hitting out and blustering advice to run or at least to get out of the way. But the crowd rounded on them intrigued, gesturing at the masks: "Look, it's the Artisans' Guild! They've all gone crazy." And when the artisans, breathlessly blaspheming, laid about them with sticks and fists, the crowd responded in kind. A spectacular fight began.

Tanaquil, about eighty feet behind, took her eyes from the

upheaval. She saw the unicorn had stopped, clear as the statues in the lights of the avenue. The surging crowd seemed not to see it there. "No," said Tanaquil again, "don't." And the unicorn, as if it heard and would tease her in its sublime unearthly way, turned to the side with a little flaunting, horse-like gambol. There was a garden or an alley there, and into it the unicorn minced.

Tanaquil ran. She caught up to the peeve, who was running still. And at a gap between tall houses, both came to a halt. They peered down a tunnel of dark, and nothing was in it. Once more. Vanished.

The peeve sat on the road and washed vigorously, as if it had just been running for exercise, not *chasing* anything. Tanaquil got its leash.

The racket from the crowd was now extraordinary. Tanaquil grasped that not only could she hear the fight, but the notes of cheers and whistles up the street, and drawing nearer. Citizens uninvolved in battle pointed. She made out an orderly movement and the glint of lanterns on spears. Soldiers were approaching to correct the disorderly crowd. And beyond the soldiers came other lights, drums, the roll of wheels.

"It's a procession," said Tanaquil.

She went forward cautiously.

The flailing artisans and their assailants were now mixed up with scolding soldiers in burnished mail and plumed helmets. The riot had spilled out into the avenue. Suddenly the whole mob unravelled and flooded right across the roadway.

Tanaquil pulled herself up onto the plinth of a lamp, while the peeve scurried up the pole.

Artisans and crowd members were rolling on the road, soldiers were ladling out blows with spear butts, and an entire row of drummers was falling over them with shrieks, while horses reared and chariots upended, and flowers and fires whirled through the air.

"It's not a procession any more," remarked Tanaquil.

She was gazing with wonder at the chaotic muddle, which seemed unlikely ever to be sorted out, when a surprisingly intact chariot shot straight out of the mess and pulled up smartly close beneath Tanaquil's plinth.

The chariot was small, painted and gilded and garlanded with flowers, and drawn by two small white horses. The driver was a girl perhaps a year younger than Tanaquil. She had long ropes of very black hair, and a cloak of red velvet and pure gold tissue that seemed to be embroidered with rubies.

"What," shouted the girl in a penetrating, high, and regal voice, "is this disgusting silliness?"

At once there was a hush. The fighting on the roadway ceased. The combatants, where able, detached themselves. Removing masks, holding cloths to bleeding noses, they stood about looking cowed.

She's that important, then, thought Tanaquil. And staring down at the girl, Tanaquil had the most curious feeling she had seen her before.

"Well?" said the girl, still theatrically, but more quietly, now there was silence. "What are your excuses?"

"Ma'am, these rowdies just rushed out in front of us," said a stylish officer of the soldiers.

"Obviously," said the girl. On her head was a goldwork cap with a red feather. "You," she added to Vush. Vush got up, his mask half off and a black eye glaring above his beard. "You're the Master Artisan, aren't you?"

"Yuff," admitted Vush through a split lip.

"What was the meaning of this affray?"

An expression of despair crossed Vush's swelling face. He squared his big shoulders.

"We were chafed by a uniborn, your highnuff."

"A what?"

"A uniborn."

"He means a unicorn, madam," said the officer. He gave a stagey laugh. "Really!"

"Where is it?" said the girl. She looked round with genuine fascination. "Are you making this up?"

"*No,* your highnuff. The Fabred Beaft manifufted among uff." Vush said in a dreadful voice, "Doom. It meanf the end."

A sigh passed over the crowd. Tanaquil saw here and there the making of signs against evil and ill fortune.

"The Sacred Beast," said the girl, "*if* ever it were to return to us, would offer its loyalty to my father, Prince Zorander. We've nothing to fear. As for you, I believe you were all drunk at some artisans' rite. You scared yourselves into seeing things and then ran out here and caused this disturbance. My father will doubtless fine your guild. Look forward to *that,* and stop spreading unwise rumors of unicorns."

The artisans drooped. They had been atrociously embarrassed. Hints of doubt were murmuring between them. *Had* they imagined the unicorn?

Then a thin, cranky artisan stamped his foot on the road, and thrust a skinny finger at the lamp standard, the perch of Tanaquil and the peeve.

"*She's* the trouble maker. She's a witch. She made us see things," howled Jope.

Every head turned. Every face for a mile, it felt to her, was raised to Tanaquil's own. Including the face of the Prince's daughter below.

The Princess frowned. For a minute she might have been puzzled, possibly by the apparition of the peeve, hanging by one paw and its tail from the lantern hook.

"This girl?" asked the Princess.

Vush said heavily, "Fhe fneabed into our hall difguifed af a boy. Fhe profaned a ritual—"

The Princess interrupted. She said directly to Tanaquil: "What have you got to say?"

"I'm not a witch," said Tanaquil promptly. She stared at the girl and caught herself back. "Of course there wasn't a unicorn. Because I can mend things they tried to force me to join their guild. They threatened to drown me if I didn't."

"Oh, yes," said the Princess. "Father *will* be interested."

The artisans muttered. The officer glanced at them and they stopped.

"Then," said Tanaquil, "they went quite mad and ran out into the street screaming about sacred beasts. I'm a stranger to this city. I'm not impressed."

"Of course not," said the girl. She looked at the soldiers. "Clear the road, please."

Order came after all. The other vehicles were righting themselves, the soldiers herding artisans and citizens out of the way. As Vush was deposited at the roadside there were jibes and laughter.

The Princess said to Tanaquil, "Come down and get into my chariot. You can bring your animal."

Tanaquil said, "I'm sure I don't merit the honor."

"It's not an honor," said the Princess. "It's an invitation."

Tanaquil got down from the lion, and the peeve slithered after her. They climbed into the chariot of flowers, and the Princess flared her reins. The small white horses darted off, straight through the loiterers on the road, who tumbled aside.

A few flakes of snow, unusual in the city, spotted the air.

"By the way, I'm sorry, but Father won't fine the artisans. It

would be useless trying to persuade him. It talks, doesn't it?"
said the Princess. "The animal."

"I can, er, *make* it seem to."

"Good. I thought you'd be all right."

They sped out of the avenue of lions into an avenue lined by
gilded, lantern-lit dolphins. Then they raced to the foot of a hill
and roared up it. The peeve wrapped itself round Tanaquil's leg
and clawed her. "Too fast. Want get off."

"That's excellent," congratulated the Princess.

"Ow. Thank you."

Over the top of the hill, where the road was lined by
lantern-lit gilded octopuses and camels alternately, appeared a
peculiar white, lighted mountain.

"My father's palace," said the Princess, faintly bored.

As the chariot slowed, Tanaquil tried and succeeded in count-
ing the lines of windows, balconies. There were fifteen stories.

"You can use that room, if you like it," said the Princess.
Her name was Lizra, she had revealed. "Have a bath and choose
one of those dresses in the cedarwood closet. Then we'll go down
to dinner. It goes on for hours. Won't matter if we're late."

She had thrown off her cloak, and sat about in a red gown
with gold buttons.

On their entering her bedchamber, Tanaquil had been half
affronted, half delighted. It was a colossal room, and every wall
was painted like a beautiful garden of fruit trees and flowers, with
a flamingo lake whose water was inlaid lapis lazuli that seemed to
reflect and ripple. On the blue ceiling were a gold sun and a silver
moon and some copper and platinum planets that moved about in
appropriate positions. When Lizra pulled a golden handle by the
bed, three white clockwork doves flew over. The bed itself was in
the shape of a conch shell, plated in mother-of-pearl. There were
no fireplaces. Pipes of hot water, it seemed, ran under the floor
and behind the walls from furnaces in the basement.

The peeve, too, was overwhelmed. It immediately laid some
dung on a woven-gold rug, then folded the rug over the misde-
meanor like a nasty pancake.

Tanaquil expected death at once, but Lizra only took the rug
and dropped it out of the window ten stories down to the gardens
below. "Someone will find it, put the dung on the flowers, clean
the rug, then bring it back."

Nevertheless, she showed Tanaquil and the peeve a marble

bathroom, to which a large tray of earth had already been brought.

The other room led from the bedchamber. It was colored like a rose, and in it were a fireplace and a bed, both with columns of cinnabar. "It's where my visitors stay," said Lizra airily, "friends."

Tanaquil raised her eyebrows. "You're too kind. Surely you don't honor me by thinking of me as a friend?"

"Are you an enemy then?" asked Lizra, with a knife-like glance.

Tanaquil said, "I only meant—"

"Don't mind me," said Lizra. She watched the peeve in the bathroom, in a delayed reaction, scraping dirt out of the tray all over the floor. "Make it say something," said Lizra. "I think it wants to."

"Buried it," said the peeve. "Clever me."

"Yes," said Lizra. "I thought so."

Tanaquil bathed in a bath where she could have swum, had she known how. There were jade ducks that floated full of soap, and a fish, when you tilted it, sluiced you with warm water.

From her closet Lizra chose for Tanaquil a gown of lion-yellow silk. It was ornate and boned, like the red gown. "We're the same size. Just as well. You have to be formal here, particularly for dinner. So many rules, like the procession."

Lizra had been driving through the city to "inspire the people." "Father says it does," said Lizra, "but half of them don't take any notice. Why should they? I have to go round once a month. *He* only bothers with the festivals. It makes you sick."

"What does your mother say?"

"My mother's dead," said Lizra briskly. "Don't tell me you're sorry or how awful, because you never knew her, and neither did I, properly. It happened when I was only five."

But Tanaquil had actually paused to visualize a life from the age of five without a mother—or without the only mother she could imagine, Jaive.

"We'll go down then, Tanaquil," said Lizra.

"Will your father want to know who I am?"

"He'll assume, if he notices either of us, that you're some royal person from another city he's agreed to allow on a visit. It happens a lot. I usually find those girls stuck-up or stupid. On the other hand, I was once friends with a road-sweeper's daughter, Yilli, and she came here often. I really liked her. Then she tried to cut my throat one morning. She wanted to steal some of my jewelry, which I hate anyway. She could have had it. I've avoided friends since then."

Tanaquil was shocked into weird sympathy. She could see it all, the sweeper's daughter's painful jealousy, Lizra's bold, blind trust, her own shock, the emotional wound she thought she should be casual about.

"I still sometimes catch sight of her," said Lizra bleakly. "She bakes pies in the Lion Market."

Tanaquil realized she might have eaten one of these pies. She said, "You mean you let her go?"

"I held her upside down out of the window first."

Tanaquil said, "Are you in fact warning me to be careful? Since you don't know anything about me—"

"So what?" said Lizra. "I just think I might like to *know* you, not *about* you. Yes, poor Yilli was my mistake. But you have to take risks."

"Yes," said Tanaquil

"Bring your peeve. It'll like dinner."

They went down to the dining hall in the Flying Chair. The peeve did not enjoy this, as it had not enjoyed coming up in it.

Several flights of marble stairs, with vast landings, ran up and down through the fifteen stories of the palace. For each flight there was also a Flying Chair. It was like a birdcage with bars of gilded iron, and inside was a bench with cushions. You entered, sat, and rang a golden bell in the floor of the cage. This communicated to gangs of servants at the bottom and top of the palace, and they began to haul on the gilded ropes. The cage worked against a counterweight, which was gently released to bring the carriage down and gently lowered to lift it. Should you wish to alight at the twelfth story, the bell was rung twelve times, and so on. Sometimes, the bell was misheard, but never by very much.

Tanaquil herself did not completely like the flying up and down through the air of the staircase wells, with carved pillars, balustrades, and windows sliding by in the other direction. The gang of Chair servants could sometimes be seen far below or above, leaning over banisters and grinning. All of them looked quite insane.

"Have the Chairs ever had an accident?" she had inquired, on having the method first explained to her.

"Once or twice," said Lizra. She added philosophically,

"They never fall far. Father's Chief Counselor, Gasb, once got a broken leg. Rats had gnawed the ropes. The rope-checker was beheaded."

They reached the fifth floor, that of dining, and got out to a chorus of pleased whoops from the lower Chair gang.

The doors to the hall were covered in gold. Two servants flung them open. At once a boy playing a flute and a girl strewing flower petals jumped into their path and preceded them into the room. If anyone of the hundreds of people there looked round, it was unlikely. The din was deafening. Scores of musicians played on a gallery that encircled the chamber, pipes and drums, harps and tambourines. Nobody listened, or tried to.

Ranks of tables, high-legged and low, laden with food and drink, had attracted sitters like hungry gulls. Servants glided about with enormous platters of vegetables, fruits, breads, roasts, and cakes, and vessels of wine, water, tea, and brandy. The meal did not apparently have courses. Everything was served at once and continuously. On the mosaic floor, flowers lay crushed. Sleek dogs, cats, and monkeys, with collars of silver and jewels, roamed the area, while on several of the great golden chandeliers, pet parrots swung, eating something or singeing themselves on the candles. A pink bird dived overhead, trailing a leash of crystals. The peeve made to spring, and Tanaquil held it down. The bird settled in a cut-glass tureen of presumably cool soup, and began to splash and preen.

The Prince's table was at the end of the endless chamber, amid an indoor arbor of vines and potted trees, the branches hung with small gems, glittering. The table itself was of gold, and of an odd coiling and twisting shape, like the bends of a river. About seventy people were seated at it in one curve or another. They were all dressed in incredible clothing, many flamboyant styles, armored by precious metal and stones.

"There's father," said Lizra. "And that's Gasb, with the hat like an owl."

Tanaquil saw the hat first. It was made of feathers, the spread wings extending over the Counsellor's head to either side, the savage face coming down to mask his eyes and shield his nose with a beak of gold. Whatever he truly was, the contraption made him look both absurd and rapaciously cruel. Of the Prince, Tanaquil had only a fleeting glimpse before Lizra had turned her aside into one of the bends of the table: a man with very black, long, curled hair, a diadem with diamonds, patchwork clothes of silk, cloth-of-gold, and the hides and furs of a great many animals, which might otherwise have been living their own lives.

"Have some of this," said Lizra. "Let the peeve on the table if it wants. Look, there's Lady Orchid's marmoset in the pie."

Tanaquil began to eat. The food was good, though some of it highly spiced. The nobles of the Prince's court were also constantly shaking out clouds of pepper, salt, and cinnamon onto their plates, and dipping sugars and essences into their cups. Occasionally, Tanaquil got another look at Lizra's father. He was a handsome man. He never smiled. And though he paid no heed to the general antics, when the clean, dainty marmoset pattered close, he pushed it roughly away, and Lady Orchid might be seen creasing her glorious gown in bows of apology.

Lizra seemed to have no connection to her father. She glanced about and spoke of several people at the table. She pointed out a lord who had invented a strain of rose that would shrink into the soil at sunset, and thereby not need to be protectively covered every night by gardeners against the frosts, and a lady who had won a chariot race, and a general in golden mail who was said to have eaten a crocodile. But of Prince Zorander Lizra said nothing. *There's nothing between them,* thought Tanaquil. *As I had nothing with Jaive.* Then she and Lizra started to laugh again at something, and Tanaquil heard herself with surprise. *Who does she remind me of?*

"Do you know," Lady Orchid's voice broke out in loud, self-conscious tones, as she tied the marmoset's emerald leash to her chair, "a unicorn has been seen again in the city."

Tanaquil felt as if a stream of boiling cold water were being poured down her spine.

"A unicorn? Some foolishness—"

"No, there were various reports on Lion and Lynx Streets. About midnight a ghostly shape went by with a blazing silver horn."

"I heard the creature was scarlet and had fiery eyes," said a noble to Lady Orchid's left.

"The fishermen said they saw the Sacred Beast of the city swimming in the ocean near dawn."

"There are always these lying rumors," said Gasb suddenly, in a harsh, owl-cruel voice that carried over all the table's coils.

Everyone hastened to agree. "Oh, true, Lord Gasb."

Somewhere above, in the vault of the palace, a huge bell rang out. It tolled for midnight, and the whole hall sank into abrupt and utter silence.

Prince Zorander rose to his feet. He was tall and commanding in his robe of dead things. He raised a goblet cut apparently from a single amethyst. Every person in the hall also got up and raised a drinking vessel. Tanaquil rose too, as Lizra did. The Prince's cold, calm voice rang like the bell. "The city salutes midnight and the Sacred Beast."

"Midnight. The Beast."

They drank and sat down. The peeve, which had speechlessly devoured pieces of meat on the table and spilled gravy, climbed into Tanaquil's lap and ruined Lizra's yellow dress.

8

In the sunrise, Lizra took Tanaquil round the mile of palace gardens.

Tanaquil was not sure she liked going to bed so late and then getting up again so early. The fire lit in her cinnabar fireplace for the night was still glowing when she woke to Lizra standing by the bed with a tray of food, already clad in a wild white gown with feathered sleeves. "Salute the day!" said Lizra, just as Jaive had made her sorcerous portrait do.

However, the sun rising on the many different trees and statues, and over the limpid pools of the garden, was a marvelous sight.

The gardeners were going about uncovering the plants and shrubs. Some had been left to brave the cold; their blooms were frostbitten and black, but already new buds were breaking, and by noon everything would be in flower. Wading birds fished in the ponds.

"Do you think there could be such a thing as a unicorn?" asked Lizra.

"Do you?"

"I don't know where you come from," said Lizra, "no, I don't want to know. But probably you haven't heard the city legends. There are two. One says the unicorn founded the city. It was carried ashore on a great wave, and where it touched the earth with its horn a magic well was formed that became the source of all the waters of the city. Then, from time to time the Beast returned, to greet the princes of the city. One day it will come back and, approaching the prince, touch him and endow him with mighty powers—make him immortal, impervious to harm, that sort of thing. And then the city will flourish as never before."

"What's the other legend?" said Tanaquil, remembering the yelps of the artisans.

"The other legend is that we offended the unicorn—I don't know how. And so when it comes back it will kill and maim, and maybe the sea will wash in and destroy the city altogether."

Tanaquil stood in thought. She pictured the ancient sea covering the desert, the fossils, and the star-bones found beneath the hollow hill.

The peeve fell into a pond. They fished it out.

"Spuff. Bad," said the peeve. "*Wet.*"

"It's really brilliant how you do that," said Lizra. "Your lips don't move at all."

Tanaquil wanted to tell Lizra the facts, but once again held herself back. Like Lizra, perhaps she too had never had a friendship. Certainly she had tried to make friends with the maids in the fortress, but resolutely they had kept Tanaquil in her "proper place": Madam's daughter.

The day was warm, and the peeve shook and fluffed itself beside them as they went to see the mechanical waterwheel that drew up water for the gardens.

As they were standing watching the wheel, which revolved the full buckets high, tipped them sideways into a canal, and then swung them on down again into a cistern, a palace servant jogged up to Lizra.

"Highness, your father invites you to his library."

"Thank you," said Lizra, "I obey." The servant went off and Lizra swore. "I know what it is, it's about the Festival of the Blessing at the end of the week—tomorrow. There's just so much ritual," she said, as they entered the palace and walked toward a Flying Chair. As the gang hauled them up with cries of hilarity, Tanaquil clutched her knees and the peeve clawed the cushions, bristled, and looked as if it might be sick. Lizra added, "By the way, I'm afraid the last three floors will be in father's private Chair. It's worse than this."

"*Worse?*"

They alighted on the twelfth landing, and walked down a corridor lined with saluting golden soldiers. At its end was a carved door, and going through they found a landing of green onyx. On a flight of stairs a band of terrible-looking people were rushing unsafely about, cartwheeling and swinging from the banisters, hanging upside down, and giving awful raucous screams and giggles. They were dressed in beautiful clothes, but were barefoot. Their hair stood on end.

Lizra said sternly, "Chair *down*."

At once the crazed activity was transformed into a thundering, screeching race up the stairs. From three floors up presently there were calls and howls, and then a burst of song—the words sounded nonsensical.

Down the stairwell came a Flying Chair of stupefying magnificence on a rope bound with silver. It stopped at the landing.

"They untie it above," said Lizra. "We'd better get in. They aren't able to stay still for long."

Tanaquil followed Lizra uneasily into the Chair, sat, and held the peeve between her arms in an iron lock.

Lizra kicked a gold thing in the floor and a trumpet pealed overhead.

The noises became a gale; the cage juddered and began to rise.

As they went up, they encountered and passed the Chair gang, who were plunging down the stairs with the other end of the silver rope, shrieking and singing something like "Heave ho, rope and woe—" their feet never missing the treads, their eyes red, foaming at the mouth.

"Oh, the God!" cried Tanaquil.

They reached the upper landing and the chair stopped rock-still.

"They'll tie it up at the bottom now," said Lizra. "Then they must wait for the next one going up or down. When father's busy, sometimes they run up and down every ten minutes. They're the counterweight, you see. It was Gasb's idea. My father thought it was unusual. They all go off their heads. They can't keep still. They have to sleep in clockwork hammocks that sway."

Tanaquil felt sick, and not only from the Chair.

Two gold soldiers now stood with spears crossed over a gold door.

"This is the door to the apartments of the Prince."

"I, the daughter of the Prince, will enter with my companion, the Princess Tanaquil."

"Enter!"

Beyond the door was a thing of which Tanaquil had heard, but never seen: daytime winter.

"Don't take any notice," said Lizra.

They walked up ten steps that seemed made of the sheerest

ice, but somehow did not slip. On either side long plains of snow extended to bluish distance, where white snow mountains stabbed into a royal blue sky. On the snow plains great cats of white, spotted fur stalked each other.

Tanaquil grimaced. She made herself recognize the panes of glass between herself and the snows.

They reached the top of the stair, and an open arch. Into the space came a snow leopard treading on taloned feet. It turned its wicked head to them and snarled, and the fur rose along its back.

The peeve lay flat, waggling its rump and grumbling.

"It's only clockwork," said Lizra. "It's all clockwork."

The peeve got up again. The snow leopard had no smell, and now indeed had retreated into a wall.

They walked through the arch and out of the snows into a great library of golden books. The sunlight gushed over the polished floor from a doorway to the roof outside. Butterflies had come in; white and silver and palest blue, they flew about the room and lit upon the books.

"Clockwork," said Lizra. She glanced at Tanaquil. "My father likes things that aren't real."

Along the roof, which was paved with dragon tiles, a painted boat was sailing, drawn by a balloon of sail wind-catching up in the air. The boat came to the doorway, and the balloon deflated and sank down. The Prince and his Chief Counselor stepped into the library. Today Zorander wore a tunic of beetle wings, and Gasb a hat like a vulture.

"Who is this?" said the Prince. For a moment Tanaquil thought he meant his own daughter, and was strangely unsurprised. But it was Tanaquil he referred to.

"Oh, Princess Tanaquil. Of . . . Erm," said Lizra.

"And *that*?"

"Her pet peeve. It can talk."

"Is it house-trained?"

"*Yes*, Father."

"Shorten the leash, please," said Zorander to Tanaquil.

Their eyes met. His were cold, like his snows, and like the clockwork. He seemed not to like her hair, her borrowed dress. She bowed, and he looked away from her. She was glad.

"The Festival of the Blessing," said the Prince to Lizra.

"Yes, Father?"

"This year you'll be a credit to me. The people expect it.

Your gown is even now being prepared. Tonight you shall have it. There are seven layers of golden lace."

Lizra winced. The Prince did not see. He stared across the library to where, on a frame, a suit of male clothing was displayed.

Tanaquil observed velvets in purple and a breastplate of gold and jewels. It would be even hotter, though perhaps not so scratchy as lace.

"Go and look at it, if you wish," said the Prince. He was speaking to Tanaquil. Cold as snow, but also a showoff. She went across the room politely and stopped before the frame. "The city offers respect to the sea. And so the cloak is made of the skins of seventeen sharks," he said. "And fringed with the teeth of twenty dolphins." What a pity they could not bite him! Tanaquil glared at the clothes. And saw that at each shoulder, the cloak was fastened to the breastplate by a gleaming, milk-white whorl. Fossils—and of such size and perfection she ached to prize them loose.

"Nice," said the peeve. It stared where she did, intensely. "*Snails.*"

"No," said Tanaquil. She pulled the peeve round and went over to a wall of books. The peeve, superior, ignored the fluttering of the clockwork butterflies.

Zorander stood with his daughter at a table, speaking to her in a low, horribly serious voice. She beamed and twittered at him. Each was plainly disgusted by the personality of the other. Tanaquil felt again a type of sickness—for Lizra, for herself.

Then Gasb came sidling up. He limped, perhaps from the old break in his leg, but it made him seem more nauseating than ever.

"Well, well. Princess Tanaquil, of Erm. How remiss. I don't recall Erm. Where is it?"

"A town of the desert," said Tanaquil.

"Ah. Now that reminds me, there was once a Princess Yilli of Roadsweeping. Have you heard of her?"

Tanaquil was soft and slightly witless. "No, I'm ever so afraid not."

"Just as well, maybe. I'd only suggest you bear in mind, *princess*, that many things are tolerated, except nuisance."

The peeve gargled vigorously.

"Talks, does it?" asked the Counselor.

"Wurrupy," said the peeve, and chattered its fangs.

"Naughty little animal," said Gasb. "Perhaps we should skin you for a brown fur muff."

"We have a saying in Erm," said Tanaquil before she could help herself, "never kick a man who wears iron boots."

Gasb straightened. "And who's in the boots? You?"

"*Me?*" twittered Tanaquil.

"Gasb," called the Prince. "We'll go now and shoot birds."

Gasb the vulture went sidling off across the room, eager for more feathers.

Lizra, pale and pouting, came to Tanaquil. She whispered: "We can go down the terrace stair to the stables on the middle roof. If we dress as grooms we can take a chariot out riding."

"What did he *tell* you to do?"

"Go and pray for the good of the Festival."

Prince Zorander and Counselor Gasb had left the room.

The two girls and the peeve remained alone in the sunlit library. The presence of the two men was everywhere still.

Lizra said, "I haven't asked you—just tell me, do you have a mother?"

"Yes."

"You're lucky," said Lizra.

"Lucky to have left her."

"Mine left *me*," said Lizra. "I could kill her for dying."

Dressed as grooms, Lizra and Tanaquil rode a small plain pony chariot down a ramp, along the edges of the garden, and out into the city. After three or four spectacular streets, they passed into meaner thoroughfares. Tanaquil saw again the sordid huts and shacks, the gaping drains. They came to a section where the city wall was ruinous and low, and went out by an unguarded gateway. Lizra drove the chariot along a road that ran above the beach. Stunted palms grew by the road, and to the right hand the dunes ran out to the ocean. A few houses remained by the road, but they were deserted, their tiles flaked, their roofs fallen in. The city drew away. Despite the sun and the blueness of the water, there was a shadow on the morning.

Tanaquil could think of nothing to ease Lizra's depression, or her own. They, and the peeve—now used to the chariot's motion—stayed silent.

Lizra spoke at last.

"I'm taking you to the spot where the Sacred Beast is supposed to have come out of the sea."

"Oh . . ." said Tanaquil, ". . . good."

"Somehow it seemed right you should see it." Lizra flicked

the reins and the ponies went more quickly. "I'm going to ask you another question."

"Yes?"

"I want you to tell me the truth."

"If I can."

"I won't betray you," said Lizra.

Tanaquil, who had been thinking of the unicorn, tensed and frowned. She had had the difficult feeling from the start that she could trust Lizra, and this had made her extremely wary.

"What is the question?"

"Are you a witch?"

Tanaquil laughed. "*No!* Good heavens, anything but."

"My father," said Lizra, "told me that witches often have red hair."

"Oh, *did* he?"

"It's a popular belief here."

"Well I can assure you, I have about as much magical ability as an orange."

"That sounds to me," said Lizra astutely, "as if someone tested you, to see." Tanaquil kept quiet. "But what about the peeve?"

"You mean the trick of making it seem to talk? That's just a conjuring act."

"No, I mean the fact that it *does* talk."

Tanaquil stared at the melancholy, sunny view. The stunted palms rattled in a wind off the sea, and sand spurted from the feet of the ponies. A ruined house leaned to the road. The peeve, glaring through under the chariot rail, announced loudly, "Rats there. Let's go house."

Lizra said, and her voice now had some of her father's coldness, "People always lie to me, you see. Or simply don't tell me things. Or they tell me things that are meant to worry me, like the red hair business. Even Yilli, you know, when she caught me by the throat with her knife, said, '*It won't hurt!*' "

"Perhaps it wouldn't have," said Tanaquil. "Or perhaps she did like you enough to wish it wouldn't."

"I hadn't thought of that."

"Rats," said the peeve plaintively.

"You don't want rats. You had an enormous breakfast," Tanaquil said. She said to Lizra, "Everything preys on everything else here. And the elegant city has filthy back streets, and beggars who are blind. Yes, I knew a sorceress. She used to tell me about a perfect world where all things were in harmony. And she showed me a sea in a desert. But she spills magic everywhere like soup. And—the peeve got splashed. That's why it talks."

"My father—" said Lizra, and broke off. "Look there. That's the unicorn place."

The chariot drew up. The peeve leapt out and sprinted back toward the ruin, leash whipping after, unheeded.

It became very silent, and the wind was like the silence given a thin, traveling voice. Heat burned from the sky and off the dazzling sea. A line of rocks rose up out of the water, low platforms that became cliffs as they marched inland. Where the beach met the waves, the cliff was hollowed out, a tunnel, an arch—a bridge. The light made its darkness seemed rimmed with iridescent white, as if fire were cutting it from the sky. It was in shape and look so like the rock hill in the desert near the fort that Tanaquil was not amazed at all.

"Do you want to walk down?"

"Yes," said Tanaquil. She did not, and that made no difference.

"Stand," Lizra said to the ponies.

They left the chariot and started over the dunes of the beach, which scalded their feet like the sands of a desert.

"The city began here," said Lizra, "hundreds of years ago, but then it moved away." They came down to where the arch of the cliff went up, its roots in the sand. "At high tide," said Lizra, "the sea comes in here. There was a well, but it's turned to salt." They had stopped before the arch, as if before a great crystal door. They might see beyond it to the beach and sky through the cliff. But could not pass.

"And they say the unicorn came from the sea?" said Tanaquil, but only to interrupt the silence and the silent meowing of the wind.

"Yes. On a wave. It came out of that archway, and struck the sand with its horn for the well. The rock was called the Sacred Gate. Even now it's supposed to be unlucky to walk through, I mean right through the hole and out the other side."

They waited on the hot sand, looking at the beach and sea and sky on the far side of the archway.

"Do you dare it?" said Tanaquil.

"People are always going in and out, for the dare. There's a story though of three young men going in who never came out again. And of an old fisher-wife who went in one end and came out the other as a dolphin!"

They grinned at each other. Then they clasped hands, and ran shrieking instantly in under the rock.

The violet shade washed over them, like a wave. The sand was cooler, clammy and clinging; it seemed as if it might suddenly give way and drag them down into an abyss—and Tanaquil remembered how she had dug out the white bones and the sand shifted—and then there was a curious, indescribable moment. It was as if she had shut her eyes; more, as if she had fallen asleep for three heartbeats or five. And then they were running out on to the scorch of the beach, and the sun hammered down on them.

"Did you feel that?"

"It was strange."

"But—just for a moment—*something*."

"Aah!" cried Lizra, "You've changed into a dolphin."

They really did laugh then. And suddenly flung their arms round each other. And as suddenly let go, stood away.

Tanaquil said, "There is a piece of air under the rock that's like running through torn ribbons."

"I didn't notice that." Lizra said, without coldness or demand, "I think you *are* a witch. A sort of witch—of some kind. After all, not all witches can be bad. It's just my father. He told me once how he met this dreadful witch in the desert. A demoness, he said." And Tanaquil, in the blaze of the sun, experienced an arch greater, darker, deeper, more mysterious, more terrible than any gate of a unicorn, yawning up to snatch her in. "It was just before he came to rule, just before he married mother. He went hunting in the desert, got lost, separated from his attendants. He came on a sort of castle or fort. There was a redheaded sorceress, and she made him her prisoner for days, before he outwitted her and escaped her clutches. She had snakes in her hair, he said. She was quite mad." Lizra hesitated. "But I wish I could think who *you* remind me of."

Tanaquil took a breath down to the soles of her feet.

"I remind you of yourself, Lizra, just as you remind me of *me*. And that's quite reasonable. We're sisters."

They stood on the sand, the other side of the arch.

"I believe you," said Lizra. "But tell me why."

"My mother," said Tanaquil. She felt tears, and dire amusement, and hard anger. "She's the red-haired sorceress. She doesn't have snakes in her hair. Actually, she's rather beautiful. She said she renounced my father, but obviously he simply discarded *her*. It explains why she went on so much about this city, and at the same time refused to show me the city properly, or let me *near* the city. How ever did she make him *see* her? Even for a minute? They're like fire and frozen stone. Of course, he knew nothing about me. And I—well, I expect I hoped for something one day. When I found him. My father. Lizra, I'm sorry, I don't like him. He's nothing to me."

"He wouldn't want to be," said Lizra. "I know. It wouldn't, doesn't matter, to him. You'd only be another unnecessary daughter."

9

Tanaquil and Lizra sat on the seashell bed and studied the monstrous green-and-golden thing that balanced on a frame before them. It was twilight. Palace servants would soon come to light the lamps. Light would make the dress much worse. It had its seven layers of stiff gilt lace in flounces down the skirt. The underskirt was cloth-of-gold, stitched into stiff pleats. The bodice was a mail coat of golden scales over lime silk. The lime sleeves were skin-tight and banded with golden circlets set with emeralds. A collar of gilt lace and malachites stood up behind the dress, with a train of green silk and medallions. There was a golden diadem with emerald stars. Just to look at the outfit made Tanaquil too hot, and gave her a headache.

"How will you move?" she asked. "How will you *breathe*?"

"I shan't," said Lizra, resigned. "Last year was quite bad, but not so bad as this. I'll have to wear it. There's no choice. And the Festival's tomorrow. Oh well, the sooner here, the sooner over. You'll come with me, will you?"

"Of course. What," Tanaquil added, "will *I* have to wear?"

"Just something flashy, and some jewels."

They sat and watched the dress, and the servants knocked and came in, and the lamps were lit, and the dress roared bright like a green tiger.

They had not, earlier, talked of the Festival. They had gone back through the arch—shrieking, running—and spent the day riding along the beach or sitting under palm trees eating the food Lizra had had put in the chariot. The peeve emerged from the ruin ratless, and darted about, and once or twice it dashed at the sea aggressively, each time thinking better of it and scuttling back. In the afternoon they made a sand castle. It was a tremendous architecture, all their adult skills brought to bear on it.

When the sun westered, waves began to steal up along the beach. They knew the castle would be destroyed before night fell, and drove away so as not to see.

They had spoken to each other of their childhoods, of their adventures and boredoms. They had managed, both, to say very little of the Prince and the sorceress. Probably Lizra kept certain secrets. Tanaquil did not mention the unicorn. It was not that she thought Lizra would disbelieve her. For the first time, Tanaquil had met someone who fully accepted her ideas, credited her experience, did not try to placate or compress her spirit. Rather, it was *because* Lizra would not challenge or dismiss the unicorn that Tanaquil did not tell her. The unicorn was chaos and unsafety, capricious, almost humorous, and terrible. It had rescued, and played jokes. But the horn was sharper than a sword. Its eyes were fire. And she had conjured it, sorceress or not. *It's mine, for good or ill.* When would it appear again? The pre-cast reflection of it seemed to be here in this room. At what unsuitable, ridiculous, or deadly dangerous moment?

Later they went down to the dinner, to almost exactly the same scene as on the previous night. Gasb wore a raven hat. The Prince wore his dead skins. Neither looked at Lizra or Tanaquil. But Tanaquil looked at the Prince and tried to convince herself that this was her father. The harder she tried to take it in, the more uncomfortable she became, the more irritated.

Lizra and she ate very little, although the peeve made a hearty meal. Tonight Lady Orchid's marmoset had not been brought to dine. They returned to Lizra's room long before midnight, and sat at her silver table playing Scorpions and Ladders, Ships and Chariots, or merely going on with their earlier talk—what they had done at five, and ten, and thirteen, and *I did that too*, or *I never did that*. The peeve had made a lair under Tanaquil's bed, and retired early. Squinting in as it slept, by the light of a candle, they saw a pair of silver scissors stolen from Lizra's room, and a small glass bottle, a string of pearls, and two or three other objects she did not recognize. "Whoever do they belong to? It must get out through your window at night."

Finally they heard the midnight bell. Lizra said, offhandedly, "Salute the Sacred Beast."

They parted with strange unexpressed feelings, each as if the other one might vanish in the night, Tanaquil thought. Tanaquil could not sleep. She began to have doubts. Should she not have told Lizra that they were sisters? What obligation did it put upon them? It had seemed wonderful one minute, and awkward the next. The peeve slunk up onto the bed with one of Lizra's jade pawns from the Ships and Chariots, which it laid under Tanaquil's chin. It had brought her a present. She thanked it warmly, and slept after all, with her head against its side.

The Festival Procession of Prince Zorander zigzagged through the city like a jewelled snake.

It was the second hour of the afternoon, and furnace hot.

The heat laid a glaze on everything. It brought out a million smells, delicious and vile. It caught gems and metal and sent blinding rays in all directions.

But the heat did not subdue the crowds, who had been up and about since sunrise.

They jostled and pranced, indulged in games and tussles. They clotted at the edges of the roads, and watched the snake of the procession slide by from avenue to avenue.

There were musicians in lynx skins, and dancing girls in rainbow gauze, great squadrons of soldiers in flaming mail, plumed, and carrying lances, bows, swords, and battle honors on gilded poles trimmed by flowers. There were standards of purple, magenta, and scarlet. There were gold chariots drawn by horses glassily shining, with brilliants on their reins and silver hoofs. There were deafening trumpeters, and clowns dressed as wild animals and sea things, lions and porpoises, squid and jackals, who bounced and rolled, played at attacking each other, or pulling colored ribbons out of the noses of the crowd. There were girls in white strewing poppies, and girls in red strewing lilies. There were terracotta camels with fierce men clad for the desert on their humped tops.

Then there came the tableaux. In one was a great ship with a spread turquoise sail, rocking gently on the backs of twenty blue and silver people being the sea. In another there was a replica of the city in gilded wood, with even the fifteen-story palace depicted, and dolls guarding it, and moving up and down on the streets with choppy doll movements, representing the citizens. There were others of historical moments, and myth. Last of the tableaux was an image of mythic history. In crimson and gold, a former prince was shown, and before him stood an enormous unicorn. It was of purest white alabaster with mane and tail fluted by sparkles. Its clockwork head raised and bowed to the prince,

raised and bowed, and toward its horn of chrysolite he extended a garland of flowers.

After the last tableau of the unicorn rode the current Prince, driven in his chariot, surrounded by soldiers with crossbows and drawn swords. He wore the regalia that had been shown in his library, the purple and the breastplate. His face was icy cool, it seemed he could not feel the heat. Down his back gleamed the sharkskin cloak, fastened at the shoulders with the two creamy fossils—old, maybe, as the earth itself. On his head was the head of a great blue shark.

After the Prince rode his daughter, the Princess, like a gold and green doll herself, in her chariot. At her side was a red-haired princess of some foreign city.

Then the nobles rode by, the ladies, and the counselors, and Chief Counselor Gasb in a hat like a sea eagle.

Following the court came tamers leading the beasts of the Prince's menagerie, some of which were reported to be clock-work, but all of which snarled, strode, and stared.

More musicians rambled after the beasts, playing soft soothing music.

Merchants and dignitaries strutted next, and all the guilds in their public uniforms, with their symbols and banners, the potters and masons, shipwrights and vintners. The Artisans' Guild seemed unhappy, and kept glancing about, and over their shoulders at the salters, who walked behind and had taken exception to it.

Last of all marched further battalions of soldiers, with carts of war machines, carefully oiled and wreathed, cannon in hyacinths, catapults in asphodel, battering rams in roses.

The crowd cheered everything. It enjoyed everything. This was the wealth and power of the city on display. "We own *that*," they said. "That's *ours*," pointing at things they saw over each others' heads once a year, and at cool Prince Zorander, and the alabaster unicorn that bowed.

From her position in Lizra's chariot, in boned silk and topazes, Tanaquil was very conscious of the presence of Prince Zorander before them, in his weapon-spiked hedge of soldiery, and of Gasb the sea eagle five chariots behind.

Lizra she did not distract. The girl stood like a statue, pale and frowning, half stifled by her clothes. Now and then she would say in a flippant voice, "Just look there," and point something out to Tanaquil in a regal manner. Lizra's public stance and face were as composed as her father's.

The sights she indicated were often extremely odd.

Not only did the procession dress up. In the crowd were persons with indigo faces walking on stilts, huge alarming masks, barrels on legs, and men with the heads of fish. There were also two clowns who had gone farther than the clowns of the Prince. They had put on the canvas skin and parchment head that made them into a horse, but the horse had a horn protruding from its forehead. They were the unicorn of the city. To make things worse, the back end of the horse-unicorn was drunk or crazy. While the front stepped along proudly, sometimes tapping at people lightly with the horn, the back end kept sitting down, doing the splits, or curling into a ball.

"Bad luck," said a noble in the chariot behind Lizra's. "What can they be thinking of? An insult to the Sacred Beast."

"There, there, Noble Oppit. The unicorn won't see." Gasb's voice, like a knife ready at your back.

"Oh—quite *so*, Lord Gasb."

"The Festival of the Blessing is to do with the unicorn," said Tanaquil aloud.

"Of course," said Lizra.

Tanaquil wished she had understood this sooner. Somehow she had not. She thought of the peeve in its lair under her bed at the palace. If something happened, as it must, she might never be able to return. Yet Lizra would care for the peeve—

They were coming into the Avenue of the Sea Horse. Up on plinths the marble sea horses stood under their lanterns, with fins and curled tails—and each with a little bright horn coming out from its brow.

At the avenue's end Tanaquil saw, between the jumble of chariots and marchers, the dark blue level of the ocean. The avenue opened into a square above the sea. The square was packed with people, and the procession flowed against them, folding to each side, allowing the central chariots of the Prince and his retinue to pass through. Before them was a high platform. A wide ramp led up to it, with purple carpet.

Prince Zorander's chariot was driven straight up, and the rest of his court followed him.

Tanaquil looked back as Lizra's chariot climbed the ramp. The square was solid now, raised faces thick as beads in a box. And the wild beasts growling on their leashes, and the soldiers and weapons of war, the dancing girls, musicians, and clowns, all piled up among them, everything at a standstill, yet managing to wave its arms, shouting, throwing its flowers, and with its sequins firing off the sun. And there, the white dazzle of the alabaster unicorn, bowing and bowing.

No way of escape, Tanaquil thought, precisely.

Up on the platform, the chariots halted. On the other side from the square the ocean burned blue a hundred feet below, and the rest was sky, with one tiny smut of cloud.

The Prince left his chariot. They all dismounted.

The Prince went out alone into the middle of the platform. He turned to the ocean and raised his arms, and the thousands in the square were dumb, and farther off, the other crowds along the streets. It was so still Tanaquil heard the clink of golden discs upon the tamers' leashes. She seemed to hear the clockwork ticking in the bowing unicorn's neck.

Zorander lowered his arms. He stood in his dramatic loneliness at the center of the platform, and in the still and time-stopped sunlight, the unicorn came to him from the sea.

There must be a way up from the platform's other side, and the creature had been led to it. Well-trained, it made the ascent itself. It trotted towards Zorander, and the crowd murmured, easily, like people pleasantly asleep.

The unicorn was a fake. It was a slim white horse with opals plaited into mane and tail, and held to its forehead by a harness of white straps, probably invisible from below, was a silver horn.

It came right up to Zorander and the Prince laid one hand on its brow, beneath the horn. The charming fake nodded. And then it kneeled, in the way of a clever theatre horse, and lowering its head, touched the feet of the Prince sweetly, once, twice, with the horn.

The crowd broke into cheers and applause, laughter and whistles. They must know, most of them, this creature was not a unicorn, only the symbol. Yet they were thrilled, overjoyed at the successful rite.

Under the noise, behind her, Tanaquil heard the noble Oppit mumble, "Look at that cloud—how curious."

Whoever else looked, Tanaquil did. It was the cloud she had noted before over the sea. It was not so small now, and it had risen swiftly up the sky, blown by a hot, moist wind that was lifting all at once from the ocean, fluttering the silks of the Prince's courtiers, the mane of the kneeling horned horse.

The cloud had a shape. It was like a long thin hand, with outstretched reaching fingers. It was very dark. There were no other clouds.

Bells and discs rang in the wind. The bright day faded a little.

"Not a good omen," said Oppit.

This time, he was not contradicted.

People in the crowd were pointing at the sky. There was a swell of altered noise, urgent and unhappy.

The horned horse got to its feet and shook its mane. It glanced about, flaring its nostrils.

Tanaquil watched the cloud like a hand blow up the sky, and her hair lashed her face, and Lizra's hair coiled and flew about under the diadem, and the robes of the Prince; the sharkskin beat like wings.

"It's reaching for the sun," breathed Lizra.

Fingers of cloud stretched over the sun's orb, and the whole hand closed on it. The sun disappeared. A curtain of darkness fell from the air.

There were cries out of the crowd, vague far-off rumbles and screams along the avenues.

"Fools," said Gasb's harsh voice. "It's only weather."

Nails of rain drove down. The rain was hot and salt.

The horned horse tossed its head, it rolled its eyes and neighed. The Prince stepped slowly back from it, dignified and remote, and two handlers scrambled up on the platform, seizing the horse by its harness, pulling it to one side.

The cloud did not pass. The darkness mysteriously thickened. The city seemed inside a shadow-jar. Beyond, the sky was blue and clear . . .

And then, from the hidden ramp, up from the sea, the unicorn came a second time. And now it was as real as the coming of the darkness.

It stood on the platform, a thing of ebony, blazed with light. And in the shadow, the horn was a white lightning.

Now a dreadful silence smothered the crowd. There were only the gusts of the wind, the chinking of objects, the tapping of the nails of rain.

Then the trained horse kicked and plunged, and struck its fake horn against the platform, and the fake snapped off and clattered away.

The unicorn turned to see. The unicorn moved. It was only

like a horse as a hilt is like a sword. It lifted its forehoof, poised dainty, like a figurine. And then it pawed the ground, the carpet. It pawed out purple dust, then purple fire. The carpet burst into flame, and the unicorn reared up. No, not like a horse. It was a tower, and the horn swept across heaven. The sky must crack and fall— And in the square the crowd pushed, roaring, against itself, fighting to be gone.

"Oh," said Lizra.

Prince Zorander had picked up the skirts of his robe; the sharkskin head slipped sideways from his own. He cantered. He thrust aside his soldiers and blundered into the royal chariot. His face was no longer cool and distant. It was a stupid face that seemed to have no bones. "Away!" he yelled.

The charioteer faltered. "The people, your Highness—"

"Use your whip on them. Ride them down. You—" to the soldiers—"kill that beast."

The square was, remarkably, already clearing. The crowd, the procession, had forced back in panic not only into the avenue, but also between buildings, and through alleys and gardens on all sides of the square. Herds of people poured over walls, shinned up trees, and dropped away.

Zorander's chariot churned forward.

The soldiers armed their bows.

The black unicorn descended, and as it regained its four feet, a howl of arrow-bolts crashed against it.

The bolts struck the unicorn. They skidded on its blackness, and streaks of fire resulted, and the bolts sheered away, they splintered like brittle twigs. All about the unicorn the bolts lay, and in its mane and tail they hung like evil flowers.

All the world was running now.

Tanaquil and Lizra clutched each other and were knocked down as one. Armored feet jumped over them, lightly bruised them, wheels missed them by inches; heavy silk and ornaments of gold slapped their faces. They covered their heads sobbing and cursing with fright and astonishment, until the stampede had gone by and left them there, like flotsam on the beach.

They sat up, white-faced, and angrily smeared the childish tears from their eyes, cursing worse than the soldiers.

They were alone on the platform in the rain.

Debris scattered the carpet. Arrow-bolts, bracelets, cloaks, and Counselor Gasb's sea eagle hat. One chariot stood abandoned and horseless.

Below, the shattered crowd still struggled through the square, but the chariots had cleaved a passage and were gone. There was no unicorn. No unicorn at all.

"My father was afraid," said Lizra. "And he left me here."

"Yes," Tanaquil said. She recalled how Jaive had left her to die in the desert. But Jaive had had some excuse.

They stood up. All the sky was now purple as the carpet. Thunder beat its drums, and the rain thickened like oil.

"It was real?" said Lizra.

"It was real."

"Not another horse with a silver horn tied to its head." Tanaquil said nothing. "And the arrow-bolts didn't hurt it. Perhaps the men fired wide—how could they dare to shoot at the Sacred Beast?"

"You *saw* what happened," said Tanaquil.

Lizra said, "Then it's true we've wronged it. It has a score to settle. Did it go after the chariots?"

"Maybe."

But Tanaquil visualized the unicorn moving like smoke through the dark of the day, through the torrential rain. The flying people glimpsed their Beast and cowered in terror. In the highest wall there must be a door. Soldiers would shoot and run away. The point of the horn could burst timbers like glass. Then up the palace ramps, across the mountain of dragon-tiled roofs. Lightning and unicorn together dancing atop Zorander's palace.

"Look at this idiot hat," said Lizra, and kicked the sea eagle.

The tableaux stayed stupidly in the square as the last of the crowd ran round them. The nodding white beast had fallen over.

After a while, when the square was empty, the two girls left the platform. Incongruous as they were in their drowned jewelry and silk, no one bothered with them, noticed them. The rain and thunder made nonsense of everything. People on the avenues were running, or sheltering under porticos. They heard wailing. Presently, on Lynx Street, a party of soldiers met them and made them out. "It's the two princesses!" Then they had an escort to the palace.

Had the knocking been less loud, they might have taken it for thunder. But then also, they had heard the clank of swords, the thump of spears along the corridor.

They had been sitting in the rose room by the cinnabar fireplace, which had been lit for warmth and cheerfulness. The miserable tension had to be fractured by some ominous act. Here it was.

"Only Gasb would bring a guard with him."

"It will be for me."

"*Why?*"

"This witch thing. It follows me around. And the unicorn—somehow the unicorn is linked to me."

The peeve, in Tanaquil's lap, dropped a piece of cake from its mouth and growled.

Lizra got up. "Stay here. I'll make him go away."

Tanaquil doubted this, but she did not protest. Lizra went out and shut the door. Tanaquil shifted the peeve, went to the door, and listened at the panels. She heard the outer door opened.

"Ah," said Gasb's unmistakably foul voice, "your pardon. I'm looking for the girl from, er, *Erm.*"

"Princess Tanaquil," said Lizra in her public voice, "isn't here. What do you mean, anyway, by coming here like this with—three, four, five, *six* soldiers?"

"Tanapattle, or whatever she's called, is a sorceress. She's a danger to us all, yourself, madam, included. Which, of course, you are too young to realize. Her trick of conjuring an illusory unicorn has reduced the city to havoc—"

"I've told you, Counselor," snapped Lizra, "Tanaquil isn't here. Go and bother someone else." There was a pause. Lizra said: "Oh no you d—" and then: "How *dare* you?"

Soldiers' boots marched into the great painted bedroom, and Gasb's slippers lisped after.

"In there?" said Gasb.

"My father will be very angry," said Lizra.

"Your father agrees that the witch should be apprehended."

Tanaquil stepped back, so that the soldiers, when they threw open her door, did not knock her over again. She stationed herself near the fireplace, and the peeve crouched before her like a snarling, back-combed mop.

The door was thrown wide, and six soldiers rushed in, their spears leveled at her heart. Tanaquil's head swam. She thought: *If they knew what they looked like, they'd never ever do it.*

Gasb slithered in behind them. He did not wear a hat. He was quite bald, and his features were still those of a bird of prey.

"Courage, men," he said.

Tanaquil gently toed the peeve. "I'll unfasten the window. Jump out to the lower roof and run."

"Stay and bite," said the peeve.

"Proof of her sorcery," said Gasb to the nervous soldiers. "You heard the animal talk. A familiar. We must take her now, before she can summon demons to her assistance."

Lizra said in her put-on, penetrating regal tone, "Before you lay a finger on her, remember she's the princess of a foreign town. Do we want a war with them?"

"*Princess.*" Gasb smiled. "She's no more a princess than that road-sweeper slut."

Tanaquil had been edging from the fire towards the window, the peeve wriggling along beside her. Then there was a soldier in front of her. "No, lady," he said, crossly.

"Don't trouble with calling her *lady*. Surround her. We'll take her somewhere more . . . quiet."

Tanaquil stared at Gasb's bald malevolence. She was afraid of him and felt demeaned to be so. The soldiers had swords; she grabbed the rocking peeve. And in that instant a lawless and unearthly cry, like nothing she had heard in her life, pierced through the arteries of the palace, down through every floor. She knew what it was even as she knew that to hear it in this way could not be possible.

"The Prince!"

The soldiers were transfixed. Even Gasb gaped. Lizra said, "Has it killed my father?"

And Tanaquil saw, somehow, somewhere in her mind, Zorander in his library above the snows, where the clockwork butterflies alighted on the unread books. She saw him turned to the stone of terror. And on the threshold, come from the rain and thunder and lightning country of the roof, black night and murderous horn and eyes like molten lava.

"Seize the witch; she must die at once!" shrilled Gasb. The soldiers started forward again.

There came a rushing whistling through the air. It was a thunderbolt crashing on the palace, on this very room—the soldiers whirled away. Tanaquil dropped flat over the peeve and rolled them aside against the bed. The chimney croaked and bellowed. And the leaping fire—*froze*. The flames were points of yellow ice—

Everyone screamed. The thunderbolt landed in the hearth, and ice and soot and bricks and coal flew out, while the room tottered, and plaster left the ceiling.

"*Demons!*"

There was only one. Tanaquil looked up and beheld that a thing with two heads and elephant ears and the eyes of frogs sat on its huge stomach and obese tail in the fireplace.

"*Come,*" said Epbal Enrax the cold demon, and cracks slid up the walls. It put out arms like elephant trunks and lifted Tanaquil, and the claw-attached peeve, from the floor. "*Red-Hair, we go,*" said Epbal Enrax. And they went.

PART
Three

10

Under the stormy sky, the sea bubbled and lashed like liquid mauvish copper. The colors of everything were wrong. The sand looked like cinders from some awful fire. The palms were black, and groaned in the wind. The beach did not seem to be any place in the world, but some sort of other world that was a kind of Hell. And out of the cinders and the cooper waves, the rocks rose up like the carcass of something petrified.

From the dune where she had arrived, Tanaquil surveyed the scene. She had been told of demon flights before, though never experienced any. The breath had been knocked out of her, but she was flustered rather than shocked. She understood quite well that she had been rescued from probable death at the hands of Gasb's soldiers. There was a confused memory of a chimney, thousands of roofs below, lightning casts like spears, and descending in a whirlwind. She grasped that this dreadful spot was the sea beach, and through the explosions of brown and puce foam, she made out the unicorn arch, the Sacred Gate. The peeve was seated nearby, washing itself over-thoroughly. Tanaquil glanced behind her. Epbal Enrax balanced on the dunes, apparently up to the pelvis in sand. It seemed pleased—mauve, of course, was the demon's favorite shade.

"Who sent you to fetch me?" said Tanaquil. A demon was at the beck and call of anyone powerful enough to summon it. Disquieting visions of Vush and the artisans hiring a sorcerer went through her mind.

But Epbal Enrax said, "*Lady other Red of Hair. Yonder.*"

There was something standing on the sea.

Tanaquil had taken it for a figment of the weather, a cloud, a water spout. Now she got up slowly and started to walk toward the violent edges of the water. The peeve rose to follow, decided against it, and began to burrow into the sand.

The thing on the sea wavered like a flame. It had a flamy red top. The ocean had come further in, and now the thing drifted inland too. It stopped about ten feet from the shore, and from Tanaquil. It hardened, took shape. After half a minute, Jaive the sorceress stood on the water. Her hair blew madly, like a scarlet blizzard in miniature. She was wrapped in a theatrical black mantle sewn with silver and jasper locusts. Her face was fierce. She was silent.

"Mother," said Tanaquil.

Jaive spoke. "Yes, that's right, I'm your mother."

After this unsensible exchange, they braved the storm and stared at each other.

Finally Tanaquil said, stiffly, "So you decided to search me out after all. I thought you wouldn't bother. I mean, after you left me in the desert and so on."

Jaive frowned. Her eyes flashed. "Stupid child! If you knew the difficulties I've had."

"Poor you."

"The unicorn—if I had realized—the magic, the mystery—I thought it was some toy of yours, made up out of bits of clever crystal, bone, wheels and cogs, your usual paraphernalia."

"I don't make things, I repair them," said Tanaquil. Jaive flapped her hands dismissively. The sea ruffled and spat at her feet. "And *must* you stand on the water?"

"Am I?" Jaive looked about. "This isn't myself. It's a *projection* of my image. I can't manage anything more. My sorcery is in disarray. Had I known—would I, a practiced mistress of the magical arts, have flung my power at a real *unicorn?* The damage to my ability was very great. Only now have I begun to recover my skills."

"I see," said Tanaquil. "You mean you didn't search for me sooner because you couldn't. It wasn't merely uninterest or pique?"

"How dare you doubt your mother?"

"It's easy."

Jaive's face wrinkled up, and a flickering went all over her. Tanaquil was not sure if this was due to faulty magic, rage, or something else.

"I say nothing," shouted Jaive, "of your coming to this city. I say nothing about the palace in which I located you."

"Zorander's palace," said Tanaquil. Jaive's image pleated, twirled. "I'm sorry. If you'd trusted me . . . I know, I mean I know—"

"That man is your father," shouted Jaive. In the pleats and twirls, all of her seemed now to flame. "I renounced him."

"Yes, mother."

Jaive stopped shouting, and the pleats and twirls gradually smoothed out.

"I can overlook your behavior," said Jaive, "because I comprehend that it was the unicorn that brought you here, and the unicorn that needs and demands your service."

Tanaquil's mixture of feelings spun off and left only one question. "Why? What does it want? Mother, do you really know?"

Jaive smiled. It was not like any smile Tanaquil had ever seen before on her mother's face. *She* is *beautiful, the awful woman.*

"I thought all along you were *his* daughter," said Jaive. "Obsessed with things, mechanical gadgets. But you're mine. Tanaquil, you're a sorceress."

"Here we go," said Tanaquil, impatient. "Of course I'm not."

"Your sorcery," went on Jaive relentlessly, "lies in your ability to *mend.* You can mend anything at all. And once mended by you, it never breaks again. Since you were a little child, I've seen you do this, and it never came to me that it wasn't some cold artisan's knack, but a true magic."

"*Mother!*"

Jaive held up her imperious hand. "Think, and tell me honestly. When you repair a thing—a clock, a bow, a doll—what do you do?"

"I—look at it. And then I pick up the proper tools—and I—"

"How do you find the fault? How do you know which tool will correct it? Who, Tanaquil, taught you?"

"No one. I can just do it, mother."

"When I was ten," said Jaive, "I summoned a small sprite out of a kettle. They said: 'How did you do it, who taught you?' I said, 'No one. I just can.' "

"Mother—"

"Enough time's been wasted," said Jaive. "The unicorn came to you because it scented your magic and how it would serve. It came as a bone, a broken skeleton, and you mended it, and made it go. It was my own thoughtless blow that fully revived it—a miraculous accident. Or did the unicorn also use me? I'd rejoice to think so. Nothing can destroy a unicorn, Tanaquil, and only despair can kill it. Once it did despair—yet even then its bones remained, and the life in them. Now it waits. For your help."

"My help. What can I do?"

Jaive smiled again. Warmer than her fiery hair, her smile.

"Do you think unicorns can ever really have lived on this earth? No, their country is the perfect world. The world for which this one was a model that failed. For some reason the unicorn strayed, or was enticed, out of a breach in the wall of its world. And then the gate was closed behind it. It couldn't return. It lived here and it pined. It died the only death it could, sleeping in the desert. Until you found it."

"Actually, a peeve found it."

"The peeve has given itself to you, as your familiar."

Exasperated, believing, Tanaquil said again, "Yes, mother."

"Doubtless," said Jaive, "the one who worked the crime against the unicorn, bringing it from its perfect home, shutting the door on it, was the first ruler of the city. To correct the balance, his descendant must set it free. And you, Tanaquil, are the Prince's daughter." Jaive bridled. Anger and pain went over her face, and she crushed them away while Tanaquil watched. Jaive said, "Accomplish your task."

"I think you mean that the archway in the rock is the gate to the other world—that it's broken, so nothing can go back through it. But I can repair the gate. Yes?"

"Yes, Tanaquil."

"But, mother, there's just air and rock—it isn't bronze and iron. There aren't any pins or cogs or springs or hinges—"

"There are. Only a sorceress of your particular powers could find them."

"Oh, Mother—"

"Don't dare contradict me. I was terrified of the unicorn. *I.* But you have never been. And now, look and *see.*" Jaive pointed along the beach. Another new expression was on her face. No longer terror, certainly. It was awe, it was youth and laughing delight. "Look and see and don't make it wait *any longer!*"

The unicorn was on the beach below the rock. Its blackness shamed the shadows, its horn brought back the light. The rain had ended and the sea was growing still.

Torn ribbons . . .

Did you feel that? . . . It was strange . . . Just for a moment— something . . .

This time Tanaquil did not shriek, or run. She was alone. The murky milk of the foam swilled through beneath the arch, and she walked up to her ankles in water. The storm was over, but the day was dying quickly in thick cloud. In an hour it would be night.

She had looked back once, and the flame of Jaive was still there on the darkling sea. It raised its arm and waved to her, as once or twice when she was a child the form of Jaive had waved to her from the high windows of the fortress. But the projected image was faltering, and like the daylight, going out. Epbal Enrax had already vanished. The peeve had hidden in the sand. Tanaquil did not know what she felt or thought of what had happened. Lizra and Zorander and Gasb also had faded. It was the Gate that counted. The unicorn.

The unicorn had drawn away as she approached. Not shy, but precautionary, as if testing her again. She remembered how it had chased the artisans, the moment when it reared upwards on the platform. The unicorn could kill her far more efficiently than Gasb. But it had poised, away up the line of the cliffs, as she entered in under the arch.

Tanaquil moved forward one slow step at a time. The sense of the abyss below the sand was strong. She picked her path, searching after the indescribable sensation that had assailed her, like falling asleep for three heartbeats or five . . . For *that* had been when she had passed across the gate, a gate that led now to nowhere because it was broken.

Going so alertly, so slowly, she touched the rim of its weirdness and jumped back at once. *There.* Unmistakable.

But—what now?

There was nothing to see, save the dim rocks going up from the water, and, the other side of the arch, sand and gathering darkness.

Torn ribbons. She had felt them fluttering round her as she and Lizra ran, going through, coming back.

With enormous care, as if not to snap a spider's web, Tanaquil pushed her arms forward into empty air.

And something brushed her, like a ghost.

She did not like it. She pulled back her arms.

She thought: *Jaive is still a sorceress before she's my mother. She put the unicorn first.* She thought: *I can help a unicorn.*

Tanaquil slid her arms back into the invisible something that stretched between the rocks. The brushing came, and she reached in turn and took hold of it.

Her fingers tingled, but not uncomfortably. The elements inside the air were not like anything she had ever touched or handled.

That doesn't matter. She tried to think what happened when she looked into the workings of a lock, a music box, the caravan's cartwheel, the dismembered snake in the bazaar. Then she gave it up. Still holding on to the first unnamable strangeness, she groped after another along the net of the air. She closed her eyes, and behind her lids she saw a shape like a silver rod, and she swung it deftly over and hung it from a golden ring.

Her hands moved with trance-like symmetry. Objects, or illusions, floated toward her, and she plucked them and gave them to each other.

She did not need any implements—only her hands. Perhaps her thoughts.

Not like a clock or engine. Here everything drifted, like leaves on a pool.

She seemed to see their shapes, yet did not believe she saw what actually was there—and yet what was there was certainly as bizarre as her pictures of rods and slender pins, rings and discs and coils and curves, like letters of an unknown alphabet.

Probably I'm doing it wrong.

She opened her eyes and saw no change in anything, except the darkness came hurriedly now.

The unicorn glowed black against the rock a hundred feet away. The fans of the sea were pale with a choked moonrise.

She shut her eyes and saw again the drifting gold and silver chaos of the Gate like a half-made necklace.

Suddenly she knew what she did. It was not wrong. It was unlike all things, yet it was right. She seized a meandering star and pressed it home—

She had half wondered if she would know, dealing in such strangeness, when the work was finished. Complete, would the Gate seem mended—or would it only have formed some other fantastic pattern, which might be played with and rearranged for ever.

It was like waking from sleep, gently and totally, without disorientation.

She stepped away and lowered her arms, eyes still closed.

The Gate was whole. It was like a galaxy—like jewelry—like—like nothing on earth. But its entirety was obvious. It was a smashed window where every pane of glass was back in place. There was no doubt.

Then Tanaquil opened her eyes, and after all, she *saw* the Gate. Saw it as now it appeared, visibly, in her world.

You could no longer look through the arch. A dark, glowing membrane filled it, that might have been water standing on end, and in the stuff of it were spangles, electrically coming and going.

Tanaquil was not afraid of it, but she was prudent. She moved back a few more steps. And frowned.

What was it? Something, even now—not incomplete, yet missing.

She turned round and walked out of the arch.

The sea had drawn off again, as the tide of night came in. As she moved out on the sand beyond the rock she heard the huge midnight bell from the palace in the city borne on silence, thin as a thread.

She remembered Lizra, Zorander. She remembered Jaive. But in front of her was the unicorn. It had walked down almost to the arch. It was all darkness. The horn did not blaze; even the pale cloudy moon was brighter.

"I've done what I can," said Tanaquil. "Only there's some other thing—I don't know what."

The unicorn paced by her, to the entrance. It gazed in at the sequined shadow. She saw its eyes blink, once, garnet red. Then it lowered its head to the ground, opened its mouth—she caught the glint of the strong silver teeth she recollected from its skull. But two other items glimmered on the wet sand.

Tanaquil went across, keeping her respectful distance from the beast, although it had once dragged her by the hair, to see what had been dropped.

"Did you kill him for these?"

The unicorn lifted its head again. It gave to her one oblique sideways look. She had never confronted such a face. Not human, not animal, not demonic. Unique.

Then it dipped the horn and pointed it down, at the base of the cliff. The horn hovered, and swung up. It pointed now toward the clifftop twenty feet above Tanaquil's head. After a second, the unicorn sprang off up the sand. It returned to its place of waiting. It waited there.

Tanaquil bent down and took up the two cream-white whorled fossils the unicorn had dropped from its mouth: the Festival cloak pins of the Prince. Which it must have ripped from the sharkskin. And long ago, had they been ripped from this cliff-side? These then, the last components of the Gate.

Tanaquil knelt where the horn of the unicorn had first pointed. Old, wet, porous, no longer the proper shape, a wound showed in the cliff that might once have held a circling whorled shell.

"What do I have?" Tanaquil searched herself, Lizra's silk dress lent for the procession. It had no pockets or pouches for a knife, its pendant topazes unsuitable, its goldwork too soft. Finally she rent the bodice and forced out one of the corset bones—as she had hoped, it was made of bronze. With this she began to scrape at the rotted rock, using now and then a handful of the rougher sand for a file.

"One day I shall tell someone about this, and they won't believe me."

She had managed to get the fossil back again into its setting in the rock base. The fit was not marvelously secure, but it was the best she could do. She had studied the Gate. The liquid shadow had not altered. Spangles came and went.

Tanaquil sighed. She stared up the stony limb of the cliff, toward its arched top like a bridge. It had been plain, the gesture of the unicorn. If one fossil was to be set here, the other had its origin aloft.

So, in her awkward dress and useless palace shoes, Tanaquil started to climb the rock.

She was glad the wind and storm had finished, for the rock was slippery and difficult, much harder to ascend than the hills beyond her mother's fort.

As she climbed, she thought of the unicorn dying there beneath the arch in the desert that so exactly resembled the arch of the Gate. Perhaps the likeness had soothed it, or made worse its pain, trapped in the alien world. Maybe it had scented, with its supernatural nostrils, the old sea that once had covered the desert. Or maybe, wilder yet more reasonable than anything else, everything had been preordained—that the unicorn would lie down for death under the hill, and she come to be born half a mile from its grave, a descendant of the city princes, its savior.

"I hope I am. After all this, I'd better be, for heaven's sake."

Her skirt in shreds, her feet cut and hands grazed, she reached the summit of the cliff.

She thought of the shell she had seen in the rock, in the

desert, held firm in the stone. Would the situation of this fossil be the same?

No. It would lie to the left of the arch, near the opening, diagonally across from the fossil below. *How do I know? Don't bother.*

Tanaquil crawled to see. She discovered beds of seaweed rooted obstreperously in the rock. With cries of outrage she pulled them up. And found the old wound of the fossil, obvious, exact, incredibly needing nothing.

She pressed the shell into it. It fitted immediately.

She was not prepared—

For the cliff shook. It shivered. And out of it, from the arch below, there came a wave of furling, curling light, and a sound like one note of a song, a song of stone and water, sand and night, and conceivably the stars.

Tanaquil clung onto the cliff. She expected it to collapse, to be thrown off, but the shivering calmed and ceased, the light below melted to a faint clear shine. She looked then away at the unicorn. She supposed it would dart suddenly towards the cliff and under and in, and away. But the unicorn did not move.

"What is it? Go on!" Tanaquil called. "Before anything else happens—anyone comes—or isn't it right?"

Yes, yes. It was right. The Gate was there, was there. And yet the unicorn lingered, still as a creature of the stone.

Tanaquil hoisted herself over the bridge, and began to let herself down the cliff again. She was urgent now, and not careful enough. She lost her grip once, twice, and eventually fell thirteen feet into a featherbed of sand.

The unicorn was digging her out. She swam through the smother and emerged, spitting like a cat. It was not the unicorn.

"Pnff," said the peeve. "*Bad.*"

"Yes, thank you. Very bad." She pulled herself upright and scattered sand grains from hair and ears. The peeve ticklingly licked her cuts, so she lugged it away. "Why is it standing there? The Gate is—" And she saw the Gate as now it was. Open. Waiting. In the spangled dark, an oval of light. It was the light of the sun of another dimension. Warm and pure, both brighter and softer than any light she had seen in the world. In *her* world. And through the light it was possible to glimpse—no, it was impossible. Only a kind of dream was there, like a mirage, color and beauty, radiance and vague sweet sound.

Tanaquil rose. She shouted at the unicorn. "Go *on!*"

Then the unicorn tossed its head. It leapt upward like an arrow from a bow. All its four feet were high in the air. It flew. In flight it spun forward, like thistledown, ran like wind along the sea.

It passed under the cliff. And Tanaquil saw it breach the glowing oval of the Gate and go through. She saw it there inside, within the beauty and shining.

And then the peeve shot from between her hands.

"*Nice! Nice!*" squealed the peeve, as it hurtled toward Paradise.

"No—you mustn't—come back you fool, oh, God, you *fool!*"

She saw the unicorn had turned, there in the dream. Its head moved slowly. There was no denial. Was it a beckoning?

The peeve squawked and dove through the gate of light.

With a sickening misgiving, with a cruel desire, Tanaquil also ran, over the sand, under the arch. She felt the Gate, like a sheet of heavy water, resisting her, and making way. And she too rushed into the perfect world.

11

To the sea's edge the flowers came. Some grew, it seemed, in the water. Their color was like quenching thirst. Blue flowers of the same blueness as the ocean, and of a darker blue passing into violet. And after those, banks of flowers of peach pink, and carmine, and flowers yellow as lemon wine. Trees rose from the flowers. They were very tall and tented with translucent foliage of a deep golden green. Glittering things slipped in and out of the leaves. The plain of flowers and trees stretched far away, and miles off were mountains dissolving in the blue of the sky. A single slender path of blossomy clouds crossed this sky, like feathers left behind. The sun burned high. Its warmth bathed everything, like honey, and its gentle light that was clear as glass. Even the waves did not flash, and yet they shone as if another sun were in the depths of the sea. And all about the sun of the sky, great day stars gleamed like a diamond net.

One of the birds slid from a tree that overhung the ocean. It wriggled down into the water. It was a fish. It circled Tanaquil once, where she stood in the shallows, then swam incuriously away.

She looked behind her. The shining sea returned to the horizon. Sea things were playing there, and spouts of water sparkled. A few inches above the surface of the waves, not three feet from her, a leaden egg floated in the air. It was the Gate.

I should close it. No. I shouldn't be here—I have to go back—

The Gate was blank and uninviting. It did not seem to her anything would want to go near it. Even the fish, now plopping like silver pennies from the trees, swam wide of the place.

She looked forward again. The peeve, which somehow itself knew how to swim, had followed its pointed nose to the shore, emerged, and now rolled about in the flowers. They were not crushed. They gave way before it and danced upright when it had passed.

On the plain, the unicorn galloped, swerved, leapt and seemed to fly, a streak of golden-silver blackness, while the sun unwound rainbows from its horn.

"This water can't be salt," said Tanaquil, "or else it's a harmless salt. The flowers don't die."

She waded out of the shallows and stood among the flowers. Their perfume was fresh and clear, like the light. She moved her feet, and the flowers she had stood upon coiled springily upright.

"We should go back," Tanaquil said to the peeve.

The peeve rolled in the flowers.

Tanaquil did not want to go back. If this was the perfect world, she wanted to see it.

Birds sang from the trees. It was not that their songs were more beautiful than the beautiful songs of earth, yet they had a clarity without distraction. The air was full of a sort of happiness, or some other benign power having no name. To breathe it made you glad. Nothing need worry you. No pain of the past, no fear for the future. No self-doubt. No lack of trust. Everything would be well, now and for always. Here.

The unicorn had used up its bounds and leaps for the present. It moved in a tender measure through the flowers, going away now, inland. And once, it glanced toward the shore.

They went after it, without haste, or reluctance.

Not only birds sang.

As they walked over the plain through the silk of the flowers, a murmuring like bees . . . There were orchards on the plain, apple and damson, fig and orange, quince and olive. The fragrant trees rose to giant size, garlanded with leaves and fruit. And the fruit burned like suns and jewels. Not thinking, Tanaquil reached her hand towards a ruby apple, and it quivered against her fingers. It lived. Never disturbed, never plucked, never devoured. It *sang*.

"Oh, listen, peeve. *Listen*."

And the peeve looked up in inquisitive surprise.

"Insect."

"No, it's the apple. It's singing."

No fruit had fallen. Perhaps it never would. As they went in among the trees, the whispering thrumming notes increased.

Each species had a different melody; each blended with the others.

When they came out of the great fragrant orchard, there were deer cavorting on the plain. The unicorn had moved by them, and from Tanaquil they did not run away. Birds flew overhead, sporting on the air currents in the sun.

"What do they eat? Perhaps the air feeds them, and the scents, they're so good."

The peeve stalked the deer, who whirled and cantered back, playing, but the peeve took fright and raced to Tanaquil.

"They won't hurt you."

"Big," said the peeve, with belated respect.

The sun and the day stars crossed the sky above them.

They must have walked for three or four hours, and Tanaquil was not tired. She was not hungry. The peeve showed signs only of vast interest in everything. She had been nervous that it might try to dig something up, nibble something, or lift its leg among the flowers. But none of these needs apparently occurred to it.

In what was probably the fifth hour, the plain reached its brink and unfolded over, down toward a lake of blue tourmaline. A forest lay beyond, and in and out went the flaming needles of parrots. Tanaquil saw animals basking at the lakeside. The unicorn, a quarter of a mile ahead, stepped peacefully among them. They turned to see, flicked their tails and yawned. They knew unicorns, evidently.

"Are they—? Yes, they're lions. And look, peeve."

The peeve looked. Tanaquil was not sure it realized what the picture meant. The pride of tawny lions had mingled and lazily lain down with a small flock of sheep. Some had adopted the same position, forelegs tucked under and heads raised. Others slept against each other's flanks. Some lambs chased lion cubs along the lakeshore, bleating sternly. They all fell over in a heap, pelt and fleece, and started to wash each other.

Tanaquil felt no misgiving as she and the peeve also descended among the lions. And they paid her no special attention. The sheep bleated softly, and one of the sleeping cats snored. The sheep were not grazing on anything. She saw how alike were the faces of the lions and the sheep, their high-set eyes and long noses.

The unicorn walked on, circling the shore.

A leopard stretched over the bough of a huge cedar. It stared at them from calm lighted eyes.

Swans swam across the lake mirror.

They passed a solitary apple tree, singing, its trunk growing from the water.

"Insect," said the peeve.

In the forest were massive cypresses, ilexes, magnolias. In sun-bathed clearings orchids grew in mosaic colors. Deer moved like shadows, and lynxes sat in the shade while mice ambled about between their paws. The parrots screamed with laughter. Monkeys hung overhead like brown fruit. Ferns of drinkable green burst from the mouths of wild fountains. Water lilies paved the pools. There were butterflies in the forest, and bees spiraled the red-amber trunk of a pine. *Do they have a sting?* Snakes like trickles of liquid metal poured through the undergrowth.

The unicorn might be seen walking before them down the aisles of the forest. It no longer appeared fantastic. Here, it was only right.

When they came from the forest they were high up again, and turning, Tanaquil saw the country she had traveled flowing away behind them. The mountains had drawn nearer, and the sun and its attendant stars were lower in the sky. A rose-gold light, like that of a flawless late summer afternoon, held the world as though inside a gem. Again, as with everything, it was not that she had never seen such light the other side of the Gate. It was that here nothing threatened or came between her and the light. In Tanaquil's world, the best of things might have a tinge of sadness or unease. Nothing was sure, or quite safe. The light of the perfect world was the light of absolute truth. And Tanaquil, who had yearned in Jaive's fortress for order, adventure, and change, knew that here there were other things. To be happy would not become sickly. To be at peace would not bore. Happiness and peace allowed the mind to seek for different challenges. She could not guess what they were, but she sensed them in the very air. Would she come to know them? Would they be hers?

Above, on a hilltop, the unicorn stood against the luminous sky. A soft wind blew, and scarfed about the horn, and the horn sang, lilting and pure. But it was not the savage music she had heard in the desert. The unicorn was no longer terrible. It was only . . . perfect.

Soon they went on, climbing up the hills with no effort. Far off, on another slope, Tanaquil saw a creature glide out of some white rocks into the westering day. It was as large as a house of her world, and scaled like a great blue snake. Its crested head turned to and fro, and the wings opened like leaves of sapphire over its spine. "Peeve, it's a dragon." The peeve looked anxious. She stroked its head. Pale fire came from the dragon's nostrils and mouth, but scorched nothing on the hill. Like the salt of the sea, fire was harmless. The peeve got behind Tanaquil. She shook her head at it as it went on its belly through the grass. And so they continued after the unicorn, which now and then, still, seemed to glance back at them, and which had not attempted to leave them behind.

The sun set. All of the sky became rose red, and the disc of the sun itself was visible, a shade of red it seemed to Tanaquil she had never seen, but perhaps she had. After the sun had gone under the world, the cluster of diamond day stars stayed on the hem of the sky, growing steadily more brilliant. The east lightened and turned a flaming green.

Miles off, a hill or mountain sent a plume of sparks into the air, and something lifted out of them. It flew on wide flashing wings, passing over, not to be mistaken. A phoenix.

"Poor Mother," said Tanaquil. "Wouldn't she love this? Why did she never try to find a way in?"

Nightingales began. The hills were a music box.

The last slope came, and not knowing, Tanaquil mounted it, the peeve bustling along at her side. At the hill's peak, the land opened below, enormous as the sky. It was like a garden of forests and waters, all blurred and glimmered now by the flower red and emerald of dusk. And floating over it, distant and oddly shaped, was a single broad cloud.

Tanaquil thought there were stars in the cloud. They were not stars.

"Peeve—"

The peeve sat staring on the hill with her. If it knew what it was looking at, it did not say.

But Tanaquil knew.

The cloud was not a cloud, either. There were banks and terraces, although perhaps no outer walls. Tapering towers with caps like pearl, and buildings ruled straight by pillars, and statues of giants—and the lamps were being kindled. There, in that city floating in the air, the windows of silver and gold let out their light.

"There had to be," said Tanaquil, "I knew there had to be—people—but—*people?*"

And then in the green-apple rose of the sky, she saw dim shining figures, with a smoke of hair, and wings. Around and around they flew, a sort of dance, and faintly on the wind she heard that they had music, too.

There could be no unhappiness and no fear in that place, and yet, somewhere in the depth of her, were both. Such emotions had become strangers. She felt them in her heart and mind, and was puzzled. But she turned from the winged people and the castles in the air, and looked back again, the way she had come.

She had not seen before. Or had not wanted to see.

The grass and flowers over which she and the peeve had trodden, having sprung up, had dropped down again. The stems were squashed or broken, and in the softness and color, a harsh withering had commenced, the mark of death.

"This world isn't ours. Even invited, we shouldn't have come in. Look, look what we've done."

The peeve put its paw on her foot. "Sorry."

Tanaquil knelt and stared into its yellow eyes. They were comrades, they were, it and she, from an imperfect world.

"It's not your fault. It's mine."

"Sorry," said the peeve again, and, experimentally: "Bad?"

"I must carry you," said Tanaquil. "You'll have to let me. Over my shoulders. And I'll tread only where I've already—it's so terrible, like a *burn*."

Just then, she noticed the unicorn. It had gone some way down the other side of the hill, toward the enormous garden under the floating city. Its horn burned bright.

Should she shout after it? Probably it had forgotten them. Now and then it had glanced back only at some noise they made, or maybe it had seen the ruin of the flowers and grass, had wished them away. But here it would not attack, it could not chase them off as they deserved.

They had been so careful, she, and the peeve also, not to spoil. But their presence was enough. The very steps they took.

She picked up the peeve, and it allowed this. It let itself be arranged, warm and heavy, about her neck. Its back legs dangled, and its tail thumped her shoulder. It fixed its claws into her dress and glared at everything, its face beside her own.

Tanaquil descended the hill, her back to the city. She put her feet exactly into the ruin they had already made. She did not examine it closely, and the light of dusk was merciful.

She had gone about two hundred steps when she heard the

drumming of hoofs pursuing her. She stopped at once, not in alarm, for you could not feel alarm here. Yet she was amazed. She swung round, with the peeve, and confronted the unicorn, which ran at her, and halted less than two feet away. Now its horn had faded to a shadow.

In the gathering dark, therefore, she could not see the unicorn well, the gleam of an eye, the mask of ebony—

"Unicorn," said Tanaquil. That was all she could say.

The fierce head flung up. The stars on the horizon threw diamonds to the seashell of the horn. It burst alight like white fires. It wheeled and the sky toppled. What had happened? Had she been impaled? Without terror, Tanaquil tried to understand. For the moon-fire horn had touched her forehead, for half a second, the needle tip, gentle as snow.

"Hey," said the peeve, "good, nice." And it lifted its face.

And the burning sword of the horn went over Tanaquil's shoulder as the unicorn put down its head. Black velvet, the tongue came from its mouth. It licked the peeve, quickly, thoroughly, roughly, once, from head to tail.

The scent of the unicorn's breath was like water, and like light. Of course.

Tanaquil and the peeve hung on the hill in space, breathing, as if lost, and found. And the black unicorn jumped aside and flew up the slope behind the shaft of light, and at the top leapt out, out into the air, and the last of the green sky. Became a star. Was gone. The final vanishment.

"That was goodbye," said Tanaquil.

"Mrrr," said the peeve. It fell suddenly asleep.

And, alone responsible, Tanaquil resumed their retreat from Heaven.

During the night of the perfect world, two moons rose in the east together. One was a golden moon at full, the other a slim, bluish crescent. Their radiance was sheer, and with the stars the landscape showed bright as day.

And the stars came in constellations. And they formed images, not as they were said to do in Tanaquil's world, but exactly. First a woman, drawn from east to west as if in zircons and beryls, holding a balance. And as she went over and began to sink, a chariot rose in quartz and opals. It had no horses in the shafts. No shafts. For each hour, it seemed to Tanaquil as she walked, another constellation came into the sky. After the chariot, a lion, and after the lion, two dolphins, a tree, a bird, a crowned man, a snake that crossed the sky like a river of silver fires.

"You see," Tanaquil muttered, as each came up, "how could we manage *here*?"

The moons and the stars showed her the burnt grass, the blackened flowers. Never had any path been made so easy.

Under the cool-warm lamps of the night, panthers gamboled on the shore of the lake. In the forest foxes upbraided her. Would she have shed tears if it had been possible? Surely she would have been angry.

She came at last back to the orchards above the sea. In the moonlight, under the sinking starry hand of the king, the line of water was like mercury. The star serpent coiled over the orchards, and their song went on by night as by day.

Tanaquil walked through the orchards, and came under one silent tree. She had expected this. It was the tree where she had touched the apple.

The peeve woke. It interrogated the apple tree.

"No insect."

"No insect. My fault."

They walked from the orchards through the flowers. Like blackened bones, the snapped stalks where they had trodden before.

They reached the shore. She was not fatigued. Fast and grim, the egg of darkness hung on the light-rinsed sky. The Gate. Theirs.

Tanaquil gazed across the land of trees and flowers and beauty.

"Forgive me."

The peeve shook itself. Its ears went up in points and its whiskers flickered at her cheek.

"Insect."

A weird motion was on the ground. The flowers were rising up again, the black husks crumbling from them. Like a fire along the earth the healing ran up from the shore and away across the plain. She could not hear the silent apple tree begin to sing, but the sharp ears of the peeve had caught it.

A response to apology? Because she was removing them from the world and, like some unbearable weight, as they were taken from it, it might breathe again?

Tanaquil did not know. A pang of ordinary rage went through

her. Was it their fault that they had been polluted by being made second best?

"Hold tight!"

She ran into the sea and the mercury water splashed up; nearing the dark Gate she catapulted herself into the air and dived forward. The peeve clawed her shoulder. There was a different sort of night, and perfection was gone for good.

12

Outside, it was daylight. Imperfect daylight that glared, and ripped blinding slashes in the sea. The sea was also darkly in the arch under the cliff, piled up somehow, though the tide elsewhere had drawn away.

Tanaquil, up to her knees in harsh salt water, ploughed to the arch mouth and let the peeve jump free onto the dry beach.

She spared one look for her world. She was not ready for it yet. But there were things to be done.

She tried to feel nothing, though all the normal feelings—anger, dismay, grief, disbelief, mere muddle—were swarming in on her. She stood in the tide pool before the shimmer, the glowing oval, so like an invitation—as the Gate on the other side was a warning—and, thrusting in her arms up to the elbow, like a furious washerwoman, she pulled the Gate apart.

She tore it in pieces and cast the pieces adrift. And as she did so the light of the Gate crinkled and went out, and only smears of luminescence like the trails of sorcerous snails, remained.

Tanaquil sensed two tears on her face, and blinked them off into the salty sea.

She kneeled in the water and fumbled at the base of the cliff. The fossil came to her hand. She wrenched it out. And standing up again, sopping wet, she beheld all the sheen of the Gate was gone. She could see through to the far side of the cliff, the glare of the sun, and the barrenness of the sand.

"I'll do it properly," she said.

She pushed out of the arch and sneered at the cliff top.

Tanaquil had known no tiredness in the other world. Now she was worn out, as if she had gone days and nights without rest. Nevertheless, she must scramble up the slippery rock and get the second fossil out. There must be no chance again that anyone might enter Paradise. Or anything wander out of it.

She climbed the cliff. It was murderous. She hated it and told it so.

The glaring sun, which burnt you if it could, had risen further toward noon when she achieved the top. She lay there, put her hand on the second fossil, and prized it loose. With both of them, the primal keys to the Gate of the unicorn, in her fist, she fell asleep facedown on the rock.

Boom, went the surf, *accept our offering.*

Boom. Give over your rage at us.

"Stupid," said Tanaquil, in her sleep, "I'll never forgive any of you."

Oh Sacred Beast, trouble us no more.

"It won't, it won't."

The stone of the cliff top was hot, and Tanaquil was roasting. She shifted, and saw what went on, on the beach below. She had seen something like this before. A congregation of people very overdressed and in too many ornaments; horses and chariots up on the road among the palms; soldiers in golden mail. There was a sort of chorus of women in white dresses, waving tambourines and moaning. And quite near, a girl, with very black hair and a collar of rubies, was poised by the sea and throwing garlands on to it. The flowers were roses, and would die. "Stop it; what a waste," mumbled Tanaquil.

"Trouble us no more. We regret any hurt or insult," cried the girl to the sea, and to the arch mouth. She tossed the last garland proudly, and came on toward the cliff. No one kept up with her. She hesitated by the limb of the arch and said quietly, "May God protect us from the horn of the unicorn. And may God watch for the safety of my father, the Prince Zorander. And for my lost friend and sister, Tanaquil, carried off by demons."

"Lizra," Tanaquil called softly, "Don't jump. I'm alive. I'm up here."

Lizra raised her head. She was white and blank, like paper without writing. What would be written in?

"It was a demon of my mother's," said Tanaquil. "It saved me from Gasb and brought me here. The unicorn's gone now. But I thought it—I mean, the Prince is well, is he?"

There was still no writing on Lizra's face.

"Yes, my father the Prince is well. Are you Tanaquil?"

"Definitely. And this is the wreckage of your dress. What can I say? I've got a lot to tell you."

"We came to placate the unicorn," said Lizra, like a sleepwalker.

"Well, as I said, it's gone. Back through the Sacred Gate."

"If that's true, my father will rejoice."

"I'll bet. By the way, if you want proof of me, look down there."

Lizra turned. The peeve was snorting and sneezing its exit from a burrow in the sand. Catching sight of Lizra, it pounced forward. Lizra dropped to her knees and embraced it. The peeve seemed startled but not offended; it licked Lizra's cheek.

Tanaquil had moved her attention to the crowd on the beach. The courtiers only stood there, glittering and gaping. But among the chariots on the road there was a flurry of unpromising movement.

Lizra got up. "Gasb's here. Father sent him with the escort."

"Lovely," said Tanaquil.

Men were running, gleaming military gold, from the road. The sun described faultlessly spears, lances, crossbows, and swords. And Gasb, who strode after in a hawk hat.

Over the sand, like memory, she heard his ghastly voice.

"The witch has returned. She haunts the Gate of the Beast! Did the fishermen not tell us weird fires have burned in the Gate for the past three nights, and that they avoided it in fear?"

Three nights, Tanaquil thought, bemusedly. *I was only gone a day.*

She sat up, on the cliff. Something said to her, *Stay flat.* But even now she did not quite credit the weapons. In front of all these people, would Gasb openly kill her? He might.

"The unicorn is—" shouted Tanaquil—

"Don't let her speak a spell!" screeched Gasb. "Silence her!"

And suddenly, as simply as that, Tanaquil beheld the spear that was to be her death arcing toward her through the sunlight. For to a practiced spearman, the distance up the rock was nothing. And she, sitting against the sky, made an excellent target. It was as though she had reasoned all this before and helped them, helped the man and the spear. She saw it come, soaring up, as if rushed by a cord to her heart. She saw it, and imagined swerving sideways, but although the spear came slowly, she moved more slowly still. And in the last instant the point of the spear was there before her, and it blinded her with light.

So she did not see, only heard, a kind of splintering sizzle. She had an impression of fireworks and bits of wood. The courtiers on the beach were screaming.

Then she saw again. The spear, in shreds, was tumbling down the cliff. People who seemed to have recalled an urgent appointment were hurrying toward the road, falling in the sand, and tottering on again.

The spear must have hit something, some obstacle, just before it reached her.

Gasb had backed away. His hat fluttered. He threatened the soldiers, but they only stood there under the cliff goggling at the fallen spear and at Tanaquil. The man who had made the spear-cast was gabbling nonsensically. In the middle of this, the peeve pelted from the cliff base and bit him on the leg, right through his boot. The soldier howled and, perhaps instinctively, kicked viciously with the bitten leg at the peeve.

Tanaquil was a witness now. The kicking foot, rather than striking the peeve, met something in the air. It was invisible, but effective. The soldier was dashed away, as if he had been lifted and thrown by an adversary of great strength. He landed in the sand thirty feet from the peeve, with a terrific thump, and did not move.

The peeve spruced itself. It did not bother with questions, merely watched in apparent glee as the other soldiers sprinted off up the beach and plummeted into the chariots, while streams of courtiers ran by them toward the city, wailing and tripping.

Only Gasb was left. He held up his hands, warding off Tanaquil and her power.

"Mighty sorceress, don't harm me, be kind—" And as her vanquishing blow did not smite him, Gasb too turned tail and bolted for the chariots, and as before when he had run away, his hat flew off and dropped to the ground, glad to be rid of him.

"The unicorn," said Tanaquil. Because she was seated, she got up. Not sure what to do, she started to climb down the cliff. As she climbed, she listened to the pandemonium on the road, the rattle of departing chariots.

At the bottom of the cliff, Lizra stood with the peeve. She was still white above the rubies; maybe they made her look worse. If anything was written on her face, it was a strange worried smugness.

"You *are* a witch. I said."

"The unicorn touched me. It touched the peeve. I suppose—"

"The unicorn touched Father," said Lizra. "It raked him across the chest with its horn, when it stole the shells from his cloak. He'll always have the scar." It was her public voice.

"Lizra, I'm sorry, I didn't intend to frighten you. I didn't know it would happen. I mean, it's extraordinary."

"You're invulnerable," said Lizra. She bowed. "Great sorceress." It was not a joke.

"Bow to the peeve, as well," grated Tanaquil. "This is too much. I've seen something wonderful that didn't want me—that none of us can have. Friend and sister, you said."

"Everything's changed," said Lizra. She had ceased being a princess. She was small and bleak, a frost child. "And you."

"I haven't changed. Something's happened to me, that's all."

Lizra grew a little. Then she was fifteen again. She said, "I'll have to show you. Anyway, you can't go on in that dress."

"What would you suggest instead?"

"The soldier's shortish, and thin. His mail would fit you. Anyway, he's all that's available."

They went over to the fallen soldier. He had come down on his back. His mouth was open and he grunted vaguely. The peeve's toothmarks showed in his boot.

Tanaquil took off his boots and tried them. They were too large, but would do.

While the man lay unconscious they removed his mail, and left him in neat undergarments embroidered by some doting hand. Tanaquil draped the remains of her dress and petticoat over him to shield him from the sun until he woke.

"Keep the topazes," said Lizra. And Tanaquil, hearing the words, heard behind them another phrase: A parting gift. She thought of the unicorn. *That's goodbye.*

Angrily, she let Lizra help her dress in the mail. She bundled her witch-red hair up into the big helmet.

"Now what?"

"They've left my horses and chariot. How deliriously kind of them. Last time, on the platform, they ran off with those, too."

They walked along the beach. The waves plashed on the shore, hard and bright. The peeve slunk to them, and drew away.

"What happened after my mother's demon came for me?" said Tanaquil.

"Gasb and the soldiers turned somersaults and fled into the palace. I went to my father. I thought the unicorn had killed him."

"It hadn't."

"Only taken the shells and left the scar." Tanaquil held the fossils more tightly in her fist. She had not shown them, she had never let go. What the unicorn had given her was stupendous. She could not accept it as yet; probably there was some mistake. She wanted an ordinary memento. "My father needs me now," said Lizra.

That's goodbye.

"And you still feel vast loyalty to him, do you?" said Tanaquil, acidly.

"He's my father."

"Oh, has he remembered?"

"Yes," said Lizra.

It was the chariot from the avenue, painted and gilded but today without any flowers. The small white horses perched in the shafts, alert, unpanicked. The two girls got in, followed by the peeve, and Lizra drew up the reins. "Gallop." And off they went, back along the beach road toward Zorander's city.

Remember the sand castle. Where is it now?

"Why are we going to the city?" asked Tanaquil.

"Because the palace is there, and I want you to see."

"What?"

"I want to show you, not tell you. That's why we're going."

The hot mail was uncomfortable; it itched. Had the soldier had fleas? Abruptly Tanaquil felt pity for him. It was not his fault he had been driven to cast the spear.

They did not return into the city by the entrance they had used before. Driving the chariot up into some groves above the beach, Lizra brought them to the city wall and a large gateway with large stone lions at either side. Here there was a fuss, and they were provided an escort. "Only this one lad stayed with you, ma'am? I never heard the like. Frightened by a beggar girl on the beach! I never did."

The city did not seem altered. There was the old noise and activity, the masses of people going about, the elegant shops and exotic market. Then, as they turned into the street of octopuses and camels, topped by the fifteen-story palace of the Prince, they were forced to a halt.

A crowd milled over the avenue, and had gone up the lantern poles. In the middle of the roadway, a chariot lay spilled. Its horses were visible inside the crowd, thieved, being led off to new lives.

"Clear the way!" thundered the escort's captain.

A parting appeared. As had happened on other streets, some cheers were loudly raised for Lizra. They moved forward slowly.

"That chariot is Gasb's," said Lizra. She drew on the reins. "Stand." There in the crowd, she turned to a burly man in the apron of the vintners' guild. "What is the meaning of this?" A tangle of voices answered. Lizra said, "One at a time. You. I addressed you first."

"Honored, Highness. Twenty minutes ago, Counselor Gasb rode up, in a hurry. There were several chariots. Most turned back seeing the crowd here, but Gasb drove straight at us."

"We were only waiting," said a silk-clad man behind the vintner, "for news of the Prince, or news of the ceremony of placation that you, Your Highness, were carrying out."

"It's traditional for the people to have use of this road."

"Yes," said Lizra. "So Gasb rode at the crowd. And then?"

"And then, Highness," said the vintner, "not to mislead you, some of us turned the horses and upset the chariot."

The silk man said in satisfaction, "We got him to dismount."

"Dragged him out," added another one, helpfully.

"He was pelted with eggs and ripe fruit from a handy stall," said the vintner. The men paused, looked at each other. The vintner cleared his throat. "Gasb wasn't popular."

The silk man said, "Some of the rougher elements of the crowd took him away, Highness. To reason with him, perhaps."

"My father will be informed of this," said Lizra. There was no resonance to her dramatic displeasure.

"Make way for the Princess!" shouted the escort captain.

"Good fortune smile on her!" cried the vintner, with especial fervor, to demonstrate he was not the right candidate for the soldiers' swords.

The palace gangs of the Flying Chairs were having a celebration. They sang out the name of Gasb, and went into fits of laughter. The Chair rose without other incident, however. In the long corridor the gold guards saluted, and nobody questioned their fellow soldier marching at Lizra's back, nor the animal on an improvised leash.

At the landing of green onyx, the mad gang who acted as the counterweight were just as Tanaquil recollected them. If they had heard of Gasb's fate, they did not dwell on it. Probably the insanity of their existence had erased any idea of its author.

The Chair rose and the gang pounded down the stairs, whooping.

By the Prince's apartment, the soldiers uncrossed their spears at once. They opened the door.

Beyond, Tanaquil and Lizra climbed up through the ice country. On the white plains no clockwork snow leopards prowled, and at the stairhead no animal emerged to threaten them.

Lizra stopped before the archway. "Don't come in," she said. "If you stay by the door, he won't see."

Inside, the library was dark and lamplit. The doorway to the roof was shut and curtains were drawn over. In this light the books looked ancient and false. Not one butterfly flew in the room. *Does he even fear those, now?*

"Lizra . . . Is that Lizra?"

"Yes, Father. It's me."

Tanaquil had not made him out at first. In the darkest corner he hunched in his fine chair. He wore an old gray robe. His black hair, without a diadem, seemed too young for him.

"Do you see?" said Lizra. Her voice was now neutral. Was she afraid to show triumph? "Yesterday, from the roof, he saw the two men in the unicorn-hide—do you remember?—the back half was drunk. And my father screamed in terror. He ordered out the soldiers to hunt the beast and kill it. Of course, they didn't. The city," Lizra looked down, "the city values me because I didn't run away like the Procession, when the black unicorn came from the sea. The Prince is disgraced. Would they have dared attack Gasb otherwise? My father needs me."

"Lizra, I can hear whispering. What is it? Is there someone there?"

"Only a servant, Father."

"Lizra. Come here, Lizra, tell me what happened at the Gate of the Beast."

Tanaquil said swiftly, lightly, "I saw another world. Which wasn't fair. I should have seen this world first. I'm going to travel it now, I'll look at it. All the far cities. The deserts, the forests, the mountains, the seas. It's what I must do. Come with me."

"Lizra," said the Prince, in the tone of a man two hundred years old, "you're my daughter. Be honest with me. *Did you see the Beast?*"

"No, Father. The Beast's gone. We're safe now."

"If I wait," said Tanaquil, "a few days, a week—"

"My answer would have to be the same." Lizra smiled. She

was several beings at once as she stood there. A girl who was sorry, a girl who was a sister, a woman who would rule, a child who wanted to be a child. She was sly and arrogant, sad and wistful, proud and immovable, selfish. Lonely.

Like me. Just like me.

"Have this," said Lizra, unfastening the wreath of rubies from her neck.

"I'm not Yilli."

"Of course you're not. I wish I didn't have to lose you. Take the jewelry. It'll buy things that are useful."

"Thank you," said Tanaquil. She held out her empty palm and let the rubies drop into it.

Then Lizra hugged her. Not as she had hugged the peeve, with easy, immediate affection, but in a quick and stony way, afraid to do more. The embrace of farewell.

And then Lizra went into her father's library and across the shiny lamplit floor. And Zorander looked up at her and held out his hand, which she took.

"You're my comfort now," he said.

The peeve growled, a soft sandy sound.

"Goodbye," said Tanaquil. She tugged on the lead.

The peeve bounded ahead down the three flights of stairs. On the green landing they picked their way through people walking precariously on their fingers.

Don't we all?

Only one caravan was due to set out for the eastern city that day.

As she approached the leader's awning on the edge of the bazaar, Tanaquil found Gork and his men dealing with the camels and baggage.

"Well, aren't you smart?" said Gork, shaking all his discs and adornments, and striking his leg rapidly with the goad. "But still got that animal. And still dressed as a man. That's not right, you know."

"Much better for traveling," said Tanaquil with precautionary sweetness.

"What? Not married?"

"Oh, you know how these things are."

Gork was pleased. "You want to come with us to East City? I can fix it."

"No, I'm afraid not. But I wondered if someone from your caravan could make a detour; I can give exact directions, about half a day's ride. It's to deliver an urgent letter to a fortress in the desert. I'll pay very well."

"How much?" Tanaquil, who had bartered carefully with a small topaz and one of the rubies, suggested a healthy sum. "*I'll* do it. No trouble. You've got a map?"

"Yes, I had it drawn up only an hour ago. Here."

Gork took money, map, and letter. He showed her the gold watch. "It goes, never misses. And you're prosperous now. I suppose you're not still courting?"

"Unluckily, I am. Isn't it a nuisance?"

Gork grinned. "Till we meet again."

Tanaquil sat near the perfume-makers' booths and thought of Gork riding out to her red-haired mother's fort in all his grandeur. What would happen? Anything might.

The peeve began to eat some perfumed soap, and Tanaquil removed it.

The letter would perhaps only annoy Jaive. It told of the resolution of the adventure, and of the perfect world. It asked a respectful question, witch to sorceress: "Do you believe the unicorn will have any trouble there from the additions I had to make to its bones, the copper and other metal I added? Will it always now, because of them, keep some link to this earth?" Tanaquil did not mention the gift of invulnerability—Jaive might grow hysterical. In any case, Tanaquil did not yet quite believe in it. Nor did she speak of the two creamy fossils fashioned to be two earrings at a jeweller's on Palm Tree Avenue, and worn in her ears. Not vanity, but the ultimate in common sense. Who would recognize them now? "Mother, I must see this world. Later, one day, I'll come back. I promise that. I'm not my father, not Zorander. I won't leave you . . . that is, I won't let you *renounce* me. When we meet again, we'll have things to talk about. It will be exciting and new. You'll have to trust me, please."

"Leave that soap alone!"

With her own map of the oases and the wells, and the towns of the eastern desert, Tanaquil set out near sunset on the stern old camel she had bought three days before. Learning to ride him had been interesting, but unlike most of his tribe, he had a scathing patience. He did not seem to loathe the peeve. But the peeve sat on him, above the provisions, staring in horror at the lurching ground.

"Lumpy. Bumpy. Want get off."

"Hush."

They left the city by a huge blue gate, enameled with a unicorn that soldiers with picks were busy demolishing.

The road was lined with obelisks and statues, tall trees, and fountains with chained iron cups. A few carts and donkeys were being hastened to the gate before day's end.

The fume on the plain was golden. The hills bloomed. There would be cedar trees and the lights of the villages, and then, beyond, the desert offering its beggar's bowl of dusts.

Bred for the cold as for the heat, the woolly, cynical old camel could journey by night, while the thin snow fell from the stars.

Somewhere between the city and the desert, sunset began.

The sky was apple-red in the west, and in the east the coolness of lilac raised the ceiling of the air to an impossible height. Stars broke out like windows opening. The land below turned purple, sable, and its eastern heights were roses on the stem of shadow.

"It's beautiful," said Tanaquil.

It was beautiful. As beautiful as any beauty of the perfect world.

"Oh, peeve. It wasn't our fault we weren't given the best, but this, and all the things that are wrong. But can't we improve it? Make it better? I don't know how, the odds are all against us. And yet—just to *think* of it, just to *try*—that's a start."

But the peeve had climbed down the patient, scornful foreleg of the camel, and was digging in the dusty earth. It lifted up its pointed face from the darkness and announced in victory: "Found it. Found a *bone*."

CPSIA information can be obtained at www.ICGtesting.com
Printed in the USA
BVOW02s2206270813

329727BV00001B/50/P

9 781596 871625